Samuel French Acting Edition

Middletown

by Will Eno

SAMUELFRENCH.COM   SAMUELFRENCH.CO.UK

ISBN 978-0-573-70308-9

www.SamuelFrench.com
www.SamuelFrench.co.uk

FOR PRODUCTION ENQUIRIES

UNITED STATES AND CANADA
Info@SamuelFrench.com
1-866-598-8449

UNITED KINGDOM AND EUROPE
Plays@SamuelFrench.co.uk
020-7255-4302

Each title is subject to availability from Samuel French, depending
upon country of performance. Please be aware that *MIDDLETOWN*
may not be licensed by Samuel French in your territory. Professional
and amateur producers should contact the nearest Samuel French
office or licensing partner to verify availability.

MUSIC USE NOTE

IMPORTANT BILLING AND CREDIT REQUIREMENTS

MIDDLETOWN was first produced by the Vineyard Theatre on October 13, 2010, with Artistic Director, Douglas Aibel. The performance was directed by Ken Rus Schmoll, with sets and costumes by David Zinn, lighting by Tyler Micoleau, and sound by Bill BC Du Boff. The cast was as follows:

MRS. SWANSON	Heather Burns
FEMALE TOURIST/WOMAN ON DATE/ ATTENDANT 2	Cindy Cheung
AUNT/FEMALE DOCTOR/INTERCOM	Johanna Day
LIBRARIAN	Georgia Engel
PUBLIC SPEAKER/GREG/MALE DOCTOR	David Garrison
MALE TOURIST/FREELANCER/RADIO HOST	Ed Jewett
TOUR GUIDE/ATTENDANT/MUSIC HOST	Mckenna Kerrigan
MECHANIC	James McMenamin
COP	Michael Park
JOHN DODGE	Linus Roache
LANDSCAPER/GROUND CONTROL/ MAN ON DATE/JANITOR	Pete Simpson
SWEETHEART	Olivia Scott

CHARACTERS

(in order of appearance)

PUBLIC SPEAKER – male, 40s-60s

COP – male, 30s-50s

MRS. SWANSON – female, late 30s

JOHN DODGE – male, late 30s-40s

MECHANIC – male, late 20s-30s

LIBRARIAN – female, 50s-60s

TOUR GUIDE – female, 20s-30s

MALE TOURIST – 30-40s

FEMALE TOURIST – 30-40s

GREG – 40s-60s

AUNT – female, 40s-50s

SWEETHEART – female, teens to early 20s

MAN – 20s-30s

FREELANCER – male, 30s-40s

WOMAN – 20s-30s

LANDSCAPER – male, 20s-30s

MALE DOCTOR – 40s-50s

FEMALE DOCTOR – 40s-50s

ATTENDANT – female, 20s-30s

ATTENDANT #2 – female, 20s-30s

JANITOR MALE – male, 30s-50s

Off-stage Voices

COP'S RADIO – female

GROUND CONTROL (POSSIBLY SEEN ON-STAGE) – male

INTERCOM – female

RADIO HOST, SCIENCE SHOW – male

RADIO HOST, CLASSICAL MUSIC SHOW – female

There is opportunity for double-casting of roles, but this should be done as unobtrusively as possible, and not for the purpose of commenting on the nature of any of the characters.

SETTING

ACT ONE

    Window of Mrs. Swanson's house and Window of John Dodge's house

    Library

    Town Square

    Outer Space

    Mrs. Swanson's Kitchen

    Seating for Intermission Audience

ACT TWO

    Window of Mrs. Swanson's house and Window of John Dodge's House

    Entrance and Lawn of Middletown Hospital

    Doctor's office

    John Dodge's hospital room

    Loading Dock behind hospital

    Mrs. Swanson's hospital room

A natural and unforced symmetry might exist between aspects of the sets in the first act and second act. Specifically, between the Swanson and Dodge houses, in the first, and the Swanson and Dodge hospital rooms, in the second; and, between the Town Square and the Hospital Lawn and Entrance.

AUTHOR'S NOTES

The set and props should be such that the specified locations are immediately recognizable and there is some richness to the design, but also uncomplicated enough that transitions between scenes can be done quickly and easily.

A general note on the acting: the first and probably most important thing is that the characters should sound, as in most plays, like normal human beings, talking. There is some philosophy in the play and even perhaps some poetry, but the characters in the play are mainly speaking off the tops of their heads, perhaps sometimes thinking out loud, perhaps sometimes seeking to share or clarify a thought they've been having. A serious and simple and kind of matter-of-fact delivery is probably best. Of course there are moments of emotional difficulty, yearning, wonderment, etc., but in general, I think the play should move along at a pretty good clip, like life.

PROLOGUE

PUBLIC SPEAKER. Ladies and Gentlemen, Esteemed
Colleagues, Members of the Board, Local Dignitaries,
everyone really, stockbrokers, dockworkers, celebrities,
nobodies, Ladies, Gentlemen, all comers, newcomers,
the newly departed, the poorly depicted, people
who are still teething, who are looking for a helping
verb, the quote beautiful, the unquote unbeautiful,
whose bones are just so, whose veins are just so, the
drunk, the high, the blue, the down, *los pueblos, los
animales*, foreigners, strangers, bookworms, those
whose eyes are tired from trying to read something
into everything, those at a crossroads, in a crisis, a
quandary, a velvety chair, the dirty, the hungry, yes,
we the cranky, the thirsty, the furious, the happy, who
are filled with life, bloated with it, gorged on words,
and of course the bereaved, the bereft, and let's not
forget the local merchants, the smiling faces, the
placeholders, us, all we people slowly graying, slowly
leaving, who make all this all possible, this activity, this
festivity, this hope, this dream dreamt with open eyes,
with closed eyes, friends of the deceased, the diseased,
friends of the disowned, and of course also healthy
friendly people with great skin and congenital heart
defects, sports fans, sufferers of autism, down-and-
outers, non-believers, animal lovers everywhere, real
people people, with doubts, without certainty, with
nothing else worth mentioning, the majority of us,
silent, stifled, delinquent, in the background, barely
hanging on, running out of time, hope, air, heart,
nerves, chances, money, blood, friends, courage, faith,
hair, time, teeth, time, time, health, hope, all of it, all
of it, those *sans* everything, those *avec* nothing, who

can't stand it any longer, who never really could, gentle gentle people, infinitely injured people, lost souls, ghouls, ghosts, descendants, shades, shadows, future ancestors, Ladies, Gentlemen, I know I'm forgetting somebody, friends, likenesses, darknesses, citizens, people, hopeful people, hopeful people, everybody, every last lone dying and inconsolably lonely person, fellow human beings, breathing people, breathers, breathers... welcome. The fire exit's over there. I think you can also get out this way.

ACT ONE

Scene One

(Average evening. Middletown. **COP** *enters and strolls across the dimly-lit stage. He comes to the window of a house, upstage. Through it, illuminated,* **MRS. SWANSON** *is seen unpacking boxes, hanging a painting on the wall, etc.* **COP** *stands outside, looking in. He strolls a bit more, comes to another window of another house, upstage. Inside,* **JOHN DODGE**, *illuminated, is seen sitting at a table, building a pyramid of playing cards.* **COP** *stands outside, looking in. He strolls a little more, twirling his police baton. He arrives at* **MECHANIC**, *who is sitting on a bench, downstage, drinking out of a bottle in a paper bag.* **MECHANIC** *eats something and throws the wrapper on the ground, as* **COP** *nears.* **MECHANIC** *hurriedly hides the paper bag upon seeing* **COP** *approach.)*

MECHANIC. Evening.

COP. Maybe. *(referring to the bottle:)* I saw that. You think I'm a cop. I look like a cop, I walk like a cop, so, you figure, case closed: I'm a cop.

MECHANIC. You're not a cop?

COP. No, I am a cop. You were right.

MECHANIC. Well, that's what I –

COP. *(interrupting)* That's what you thought. Everything is as everything seems, I guess. Good for everything. What about you?

MECHANIC. What do you mean?

COP. What about you?

MECHANIC. I don't know. I mean, who knows, you know?

COP. No. What are you doing here?

MECHANIC. I don't know, I was just walking around. Later tonight, I thought I might –

COP. *(interrupting)* Forget about before and after. I mean now.

MECHANIC. Well, I don't know, because I was –

COP. *(interrupting)* You don't know because you don't know. That's the trouble, the beauty, the trouble. So let's just leave it at that. *(motioning to the wrapper* **MECHANIC** *threw on the ground)* I think you dropped something.

*(***MECHANIC*** picks up the wrapper.)*

The problem with people like –

MECHANIC. *(interrupting)* I was just sitting here, minding my –

COP. *(interrupting)* Don't interrupt.

(Long pause, as **MECHANIC** *waits and does not interrupt.)*

MECHANIC. Was there something else you were –

COP. *(interrupting)* I thought I said, don't interrupt. You know what, I should just goddamn… *(Long pause. To audience:)* Welcome. Hi, hello. Welcome to the little town of Middletown. Ordinary place, ordinary time. But aren't they all? No. They are not, all. *(to* **MECHANIC***)* Say something nice.

MECHANIC. *(to both the audience and to* **COP**, *with some unease)* I'm just sitting here. I don't know what else. Um… *(He tries to think of something else.)*

COP. *(to audience)* Right. Anyway, Middletown. Population: stable; elevation: same. The main street is called Main Street. The side streets are named after trees. Things are fairly predictable. People come, people go. Crying, by the way, in both directions.

MECHANIC. Ain't that the truth.

COP. *(immediately)* Why don't you get out of here.

MECHANIC. *(defensively)* Why? I'm not doing anything.

COP. And that's a reason you should stay? Let's go, move.

MECHANIC. Where?

COP. A different bench, I don't know, another perspective. Just not here, okay? In fact, you know what – here, allow me. I want to help you make a little speech.

(COP moves behind MECHANIC and begins to choke him with his baton, pulling it with both hands against MECHANIC's throat, from behind. MECHANIC struggles, unable to breathe, unable to get free.)

Say, "This is my hometown." Say, "My life's a mystery to me." Say it! Be a good human. Be filled with humility. With wonder and awe. Awe!

(MECHANIC tries to speak, but is unable to breathe. COP continues to choke him.)

It's not easy, is it. Well, that's life. Listen, I'm sorry for what I'm still doing to you. Truly. But, don't worry. It'll be over in three, two, one...

(COP continues choking MECHANIC for three or four more seconds, and then releases him. MECHANIC tries to breathe, tries to recover. He begins to exit.)

(to MECHANIC:) Hey, no, I didn't mean you had to –

(MECHANIC mutters something.)

(to MECHANIC:) Wonderful, great. *(brief pause to audience:)* Excuse me. I'm not exactly sure what I was hoping to... I apologize. I was just trying to imitate nature. Anyway, welcome. Honestly. Middletown.

(COP exits.)

Scene Two

(Morning. The library. **LIBRARIAN** *is at her desk, on the front of which is a sign that reads "INFORMATION."* **MRS. SWANSON** *enters.)*

MRS. SWANSON. Good morning. I was hoping to get a library card.

LIBRARIAN. Good for you, dear. I think a lot of people figure, "Why bother? I'm just going to die, anyway." Let me just find the form. *(She looks through some paperwork.)*

MRS. SWANSON. I wanted to learn more about the area. Do you have any books on Middletown?

LIBRARIAN. I should certainly hope so – let me take a look.

(She searches on her computer, believes for a moment that she's found something.)

And... *voila.* Oops – no, sorry, we don't. There's a wonderful book called Yesteryear in Today's City of Tomorrow. But it's out. It's due next Tuesday.

*(***MECHANIC** *enters.)*

Hello.

*(***MECHANIC** *heads toward a magazine rack or a chair. His voice is somewhat hoarse:)*

MECHANIC. Hi.

LIBRARIAN. *(searching on her computer)* Here's something from the Chamber of Commerce, just to give you a general sense. *(She reads from the screen:)* "Middletown was built on the ruins of other older Middletowns, and, before them, a town called Middenton, which was named for being between two other places, both unknown and now incidentally gone." *(stops reading)* That doesn't sound right. "Incidentally gone." Anyway *(She returns to reading:)*, "A thousand years ago, the area was home to the Chakmawg Indian and it was called Inpetway, which no one knows what it means, but it might have meant, 'You are far away' or, 'Far away from me.' The Chakmawg had a highly developed culture and they thrived in their time, until they disappeared, forever. New residents arrived and looked around." *(stops reading)* That's not much of a sentence. But I guess it still helps to give us a picture – people kind of lost and smiling. But, okay, let's see, *(She re-finds her place in the text and continues reading:)* "...arrived and looked around. Today, Middletown is a beehive, a human beehive, of activity and business. Many come to raise families and watch, swollen with civic pride, as their baby draws its first breath of local air. Also, drawn by the excellent clouds and the mostly silent nights, many come here to quietly retire. Middletown. We've got you coming and going."

MRS. SWANSON. That's from the Chamber of Commerce?

LIBRARIAN. I know. There's a lot it doesn't mention. There's the library, here. And of course, the people. Which is what most places are made out of, if you think about it.

MRS. SWANSON. I guess. I'll wait for that other book. *(brief pause)* We just moved here.

MECHANIC. *(looking through a magazine, far from the LIBRARIAN's desk)* I'm listening in on your conversation.

(LIBRARIAN and MRS. SWANSON briefly look over at MECHANIC.)

LIBRARIAN. Sorry. You were saying?

MRS. SWANSON. My husband and I just moved here.

LIBRARIAN. Well, welcome. Is it just you two?

MRS. SWANSON. It's just us. He travels. But we're here now. I am. We're trying to start a family.

MECHANIC. "Come on, family – start! Start, you bastard!"

LIBRARIAN. *(to MECHANIC)* Shhhh. *(to MRS. SWANSON)* Well, welcome to you both. That's wonderful. How long have you been trying?

MRS. SWANSON. Almost a year now.

LIBRARIAN. And I imagine it must be about the same for your husband. Well, good. Something you both can work on. Good for you. The world needs another person.

MECHANIC. *(again, from across the room)* Whatever you do, don't have an only child. They're the worst. Or so I've been told. Every time you hear a little noise, some little singing or humming, you look over, and there it is again, the same only-child. *(brief pause)* I'm just being me.

LIBRARIAN. Don't mind him, he's only…. *(to* **MECHANIC***:)* You're just responding to things around you, aren't you, dear.

MECHANIC. Basically. *(very brief pause)* Hey, just did it again.

LIBRARIAN. *(to* **MRS. SWANSON***:)* Is there something else I can help you with?

MRS. SWANSON. Do you have books on children? You must. On childbirth and children?

LIBRARIAN. We do. They're in the business section – I've never known why. I'll show you.

*(*JOHN DODGE *enters.)*

JOHN DODGE. Hi. Quick question. Books on gravity.

LIBRARIAN. Hi, John. *(to* **MRS. SWANSON***:)* Let me just get him squared away. One second. *(Searching on her computer. To* **JOHN DODGE***:)* Books about gravity. Let's see. We have two: The Silent Killer and another one called Laws of the World.

JOHN DODGE. The second one.

LIBRARIAN. That just came back. Let me go see if it's sitting on a roll-y cart somewhere. *(She exits.)*

MRS. SWANSON. Gravity. *(very brief pause)* Hello.

JOHN DODGE. Hi.

MRS. SWANSON. We just moved here.

JOHN DODGE. That's great. Who's we?

MECHANIC. They're trying to start a family.

MRS. SWANSON. Yes, we are, *(to* **MECHANIC***:)*, thank you. We is my husband and I.

(**MECHANIC** *gets involved in reading a magazine article.*)

(*to* **JOHN DODGE:**) You live here, obviously.

JOHN DODGE. That I do. Is it obvious? Ten years, now. Ten, fifteen years. In fact, I think we're talking fifteen, twenty years, now. Time, you know? "Whooooosh." "Clank."

MRS. SWANSON. I guess. And what do you do?

JOHN DODGE. More like, what *don't* I do.

MRS. SWANSON. Okay, what *don't* you do?

JOHN DODGE. (*brief pause*) You originally asked what *do* I do. So I'll answer that. I do paperwork, lawn work, plumbing, sometimes some house painting. I've worked graveyards, regular hours, happy hours. Sure, sometimes, I'll just stare out a window, let a year go by, two years. For instance, right now, I'm kind of between things. I'm between two crappy jobs, I'm sure – I just don't know what the second one is, yet. Give a call. I'm also trying to catch up on some reading. You might say I'm bent on self-improvement, although I'm sure there's a better phrase. (*brief pause*) What about you? Wait, let me guess.

(*A pause, perhaps five or ten seconds, in which* **JOHN DODGE** *stares at* **MRS. SWANSON** *and she waits for him to guess.*)

Yeah, I give up – no idea.

MRS. SWANSON. (*following the above line very quickly:*) I used to manage a restaurant. Before that I worked in a bank. Just jobs, you know. When we get settled, I might do something else.

JOHN DODGE. You sound like me.

MRS. SWANSON. No, I don't. I do?

JOHN DODGE. Sort of. Not really. I hate how I sound. You don't sound like me.

LIBRARIAN. (*enters, with book*) Here we are. Speaking of gravity, you might be surprised to know we have a real astronaut from here.

MRS. SWANSON. I am. Wow.

JOHN DODGE. I bought a tandem bicycle from him. He was really friendly when I brought it back.

LIBRARIAN. Oh, he's a complete gentleman. He has one of those haircuts. He said he wouldn't be able to see us, way up there, but that he'd think about us. Can you imagine? All that splendor, all that wonder and beauty, and all you can say is just, "Houston this," and "Houston that." To be so far away, with such a little vocabulary. *(She stamps the book for* **JOHN DODGE***.)* And then there's John, here, with his handy-man work and now his reading. Such *lively* people, our townspeople. Always trying different things. Always pre-occupied. *(to* **MRS. SWANSON:***)* And now you, too.

(hands **JOHN DODGE** *the book)*

There you go. Bye, John.

JOHN DODGE. Thanks. Bye. *(to* **MRS. SWANSON:***)* Nice talking to you. Here's my card.

MRS. SWANSON. *(She looks at it.)* This says "Lucy Graves Associates: If you need help, we can help."

JOHN DODGE. Yeah, that's wrong, that's someone else's card.

MRS. SWANSON. Okay. *(pause)* Well, so, then, how would I get in touch with –

JOHN DODGE. *(interrupting)* Here, why don't I just write my name and number on that one. *(He does so.)* There we go. Problem created, problem solved. Bye. *(exits)*

MRS. SWANSON. Bye.

LIBRARIAN. *(to* **MRS. SWANSON:***)* Now, you wanted books on children. What, specifically?

MRS. SWANSON. Health. Pre-natal health. And also maybe wallpapering. We want to get a room ready.

LIBRARIAN. It's so exciting. A room. Wallpaper. I love the patterns. Little flowers or fire engines – it's almost too much. Let me show you.

(They exit.)

(**MECHANIC** *moves downstage and stands very still,
looking through the audience.*)

MECHANIC. I was nervous, earlier. I don't know why. Well,
I do know – for part of it, I was being choked. And
I'm nervous now, now that I think of it. But, I'm
nothing special, post-natally speaking. I fix cars, I try
to. I get hassled by the cops, try to maintain a certain
– I don't know – sobriety. Sometimes, I volunteer at
the hospital, dress up for the kids. It was part of a plea
deal. But, what isn't. Nothing really crazy to report.
Except, I found this rock once, everyone. What I
thought was a meteorite. I brought the thing into the
school, here. The kids ran it through all these tests,
tapped on it, shined lights at it. I found it in a field. It
looked special. Then the astronaut here told me it was
just a rock. Said it was probably from, at some earlier
time, another slightly larger rock. His name is Greg
Something. I had ideas about getting famous, getting
on local TV with my meteorite. When it turned out
to just be a rock, I thought I could still make some
headlines with it if I threw it off a bridge, hit some
family in their car and killed everybody. But then I
figured, you know what, forget it, that's not me. So
now some family's driving around, not knowing how
lucky they are, not knowing how sweet it all is. Just
because. *(very brief pause)* Wait, hang on a second. Do
you... *(Pause. He stays very still and listens intently.)* I
thought I heard something. *(listens again for a moment)*
I'm still not convinced I didn't. Weird. Anyway, that
was just a little local story. Although, you know, it
almost had outer space in it. *(brief pause)* I wish that
lady luck, with the family. People don't stop to think
of how lucky they are. I do. And, I've realized, I'm not
that lucky. But I get by. If I had more self-esteem, more
stick-to-itiveness, I might have been a murderer. I was
a child once. Like everybody. Some worried mother's
son or distant father's daughter, sneaking around with

a dirty face and an idea. My hand was this big. *(With thumb and forefinger, he indicates the size of an infant's hand.)* I was somebody's golden child, somebody's little hope. Now, I'm more just, you know, a local resident. Another earthling.

(MECHANIC exits as LIBRARIAN returns to her desk.)

MECHANIC. Bye.

LIBRARIAN. Were you looking for anything, in particular?

MECHANIC. No, I'm good.

LIBRARIAN. Okay.

(She returns to working at her desk. Lights down.)

Scene Three

(Same stage-set as in Scene One. **JOHN DODGE***'s house
and the* **SWANSON***'s house.* **COP** *enters, in the opposite
direction of his earlier stroll, and comes downstage.
We see* **MRS. SWANSON** *and* **JOHN DODGE** *in their
windows, intermittently, getting up to get a glass of
water or something simple like that.* **COP** *speaks into his
two-way radio.)*

COP. All units in the vicinity: see the man. See the man. See
the woman. See the streets and houses, the shadows,
the words that don't rhyme. All quiet here, over. No
News is Good News, over. But there's no such thing
as No News, over. Try to see my point. Just look at
yourself, over. See the Universe. See a tiny person in
the middle of it all, thrashing. See the bright side. Try
to look at the bright side. *(Brief pause. To audience:)*
Sometimes I'll talk like this, over the wire. Just to see if
anyone's listening.

COP'S RADIO (FEMALE VOICE). *(Very brief pause. Very flatly.)*
Someone's listening.

COP. Well, there you go. Now I know. *(into two-way radio:)*
Hi, Susan. Sorry. All clear.

*(He turns down radio, strolls. He comes to the window
of* **JOHN DODGE***'s house. He stands outside, looking
in.* **JOHN DODGE,** *illuminated, is inside, tossing a ball
up and down, making notes.* **COP** *strolls to the window
of the* **SWANSON** *house.* **MRS. SWANSON,** *illuminated,
is inside reading. She stands, referring to her book and
moving her hand over her belly.)*

*(***COP** *turns to audience, moves downstage.)*

COP. *(gently:)* I do like this time of day: night. All the people.
All their bones and arteries and personal problems.
Beautiful animal: the Person. Dark. *(pause)* I was too
rough with that guy, earlier. I think I embarrassed
him. Regrettable. I'm not myself. Sad stuff at home

and I haven't been sleeping, but, I guess we all have a story. Once upon a time, Once upon a time, and so on, The End. *(brief pause)* I try to uphold the law, keep some order around here, but, I have my moods. I just remember screaming "Awe" at the poor guy. Hard word to scream. It just sounds like a sound. And you can't bully people into feeling something, anyway. Oh, well. *(pause)* We once almost had a Glass Museum, here. It would have been called the Middletown Glass Museum. Fact.

(Brief pause. He looks back toward the windows.)

Behold. You know, just, look.

(In their separate windows, we see **JOHN DODGE**, *illuminated, continuing their earlier actions.)*

This is what life is like, here, right now. *(brief pause)* Looking in people's windows at night makes you feel lonely. Lonely, but, lonely along with the people in the windows. Along with the whole world, the whole lonely billions. It feels sort of holy, in some screwy way. Fact. *(brief pause)* Fact.

Scene Four

*(Bright daylight. Town Square. **TOUR GUIDE** is holding a clipboard and some maps. She is standing before a simple block of granite, which measures 4' by 4' by 4', and features a small plaque bearing an inscription in unreadably small letters. She checks her watch. A tourist couple arrives. **MALE TOURIST** has a camera hanging around his neck.)*

TOUR GUIDE. Morning. Are you here for the walking tour?

FEMALE TOURIST. We are. Hi.

TOUR GUIDE. Great. Hi. Have you done walking tours before?

MALE TOURIST. *(looking at the monument)* We went to Rome, last summer.

TOUR GUIDE. Oh. I bet you saw some serious monuments there.

MALE TOURIST. The whole place is history.

FEMALE TOURIST. We walked everywhere. We saw all the famous things. A lot of the ancient inscriptions are chipped off or just kind of worn away. And they're in Latin, so even if they were readable, you can't really read them.

MALE TOURIST. It's a dead language.

TOUR GUIDE. *(referring to the monument)* Well, this is in English, so people can enjoy it for years to come.

FEMALE TOURIST. What about when English dies?

TOUR GUIDE. Oh, I think English'll be around for a pretty long time.

FEMALE TOURIST. I doubt the Romans thought Latin was going anywhere, either.

MALE TOURIST. We went to Holland, two summers ago. Holland was a world power, a glorious empire, ruthless. *(brief pause)* We loved those "stroopwafels." They're, like, the local yummy snack. Ruthless empire; yummy snack. People change. Empires, too, is my point. So, ergo, I'm wary of monuments.

FEMALE TOURIST. He likes statues of horses, but, just the horse, no rider. Ergo... *(small shrug)* you know?

MALE TOURIST. I used to gamble – the ponies, trotters. I kept scribbly notebooks and had big dark circles under my eyes. Lost my job, my previous wife – not a long story. But, anyway, yeah, *(gesturing toward monument)* this makes me feel sort of sad and beautiful, sure, but not *that* sad and beautiful. *(brief pause)* Look at us. No, really look at me and her.

FEMALE TOURIST. Just because we don't look like pilgrims doesn't mean we're not pilgrims.

MALE TOURIST. I can see why you'd think we're just yahoos on vacation. But, we're serious people.

TOUR GUIDE. No, of course you are. *(pause)* I'm not sure what you – I mean, I don't know... I give this tour every day. I'm normally thinking about lunch or finding another job – I'm not really focused on the next ten thousand years. What can I say? We don't have any other statu –

MALE TOURIST. *(interrupting)* I'm not trying to be difficult.

FEMALE TOURIST. *(looking at monument)* I sort of like it. It reminds me of my dad.

(They all look at it for a moment.)

(to **MALE TOURIST***:)* But I can see what you're saying. *(to* **TOUR GUIDE***:)* I guess we kind of like a strange angle on things. If we go to the opera or something, sometimes we specially request Obstructed View seats. It somehow adds to the whole experience.

MALE TOURIST. And they're cheaper.

FEMALE TOURIST. We love a bargain. You know that saying, "Politeness doesn't cost you anything"? Sometimes, that's what we'll do for the weekend. Just go around being polite.

MALE TOURIST. We've saved a fortune.

FEMALE TOURIST. But, so, yeah, I guess we just like some perspective.

MALE TOURIST. That's right. Perspective.

TOUR GUIDE. Sure, of course. *(pause)* I grew up here. *(referring to monument)* This thing was just always – I don't know – There. I'd see it in the rain and snow, serving its purpose. So that we remember, I guess. In general. So that we have memories.

FEMALE TOURIST. That's a thought.

TOUR GUIDE. I haven't traveled, ever. I'll walk around town, is about it. I'll notice a building or something. I'll look at people. I don't know. I grew up here. I thought this was the world.

MALE TOURIST. Of course you did. But, hey, let me get a quick picture of you being wrong.

(He snaps a photo of **TOUR GUIDE.***)*

FEMALE TOURIST. We always sort of want something more, I guess because there's a long history of death in both our families. I guess we like things that are potentially monumental, but that aren't necessarily monumentalized, yet.

TOUR GUIDE. Well, then, I don't know – *(looking around)* I guess then maybe that's everything else. Technically. *(referring to the monument)* Other than this.

FEMALE TOURIST. I guess.

TOUR GUIDE. I don't really know what you want.

MALE TOURIST. Just, something, you know. You're the one with the clipboard. *(He takes a photograph.)*

TOUR GUIDE. Well, okay. Take the air. I wrote on it in school. Take a deep breath. *(They do.)* A hundred years ago, someone was digging a hole here, for this very monument, and he rested on his shovel and sighed. You just inhaled a molecule of the air that shoveler exhaled, in that quiet sigh long ago.

FEMALE TOURIST. *(slightly surprised, as if she's sensed that particular molecule)* Oh yeah.

MALE TOURIST. *(He feels he's also sensed one of the ancient molecules.)* Sweet.

TOUR GUIDE. Yeah. I mean, think of how personal everything is, ultimately – these little sighs, going around in time and space. But then, think of a beautiful sunset on Earth, before human beings had ever evolved. It just beautifully sets. No one there to say, "Oooh" or "Ahhh," or something breathy like that. It just sets, and then it's night, nothing personal.

(MRS. SWANSON enters.)

Morning. *(to the group:)* Beneath us, okay, the dirt the sighing man was digging into? It's layers of fossils and broken pottery and things they think had religious value. Maybe some sad little instrument, way down, a hollow bone with three holes in it. Down we go. Maybe a tooth or a piece of cloth. It's people strewn all the way through. Some of the dust on my shoes is from outer space; most of the rest is dead human skin.

(JOHN DODGE enters, opposite side of the stage, carrying a plastic shopping bag. He stops and looks inside it, checks his pockets.)

And there's a person, looking for something in a bag.

FEMALE TOURIST. It sort of completes the scene.

TOUR GUIDE. Sort of.

MALE TOURIST. *(taking a photograph of JOHN DODGE)* Look at him. Classic.

MRS. SWANSON. *(She leaves the group, saying "hi" to them as she goes.)* Excuse me. Hi.

TOUR GUIDE. *(to MRS. SWANSON, as she moves away:)* Hi. Bye. *(brief pause)* You know what – there's a meadow we could walk to. Just nice grass and trees, nothing noticeably historical going on.

FEMALE TOURIST. We got married in a meadow.

TOUR GUIDE. Then this'll bring back some memories.

MALE TOURIST. It really will. "Married in a meadow."

TOUR GUIDE. Okay, then. Onward.

(They exit.)

Scene Five

(MRS. SWANSON, who has been standing off to the side, perhaps trying to remember John's name, perhaps checking her hair, etc., approaches JOHN DODGE.)

MRS. SWANSON. John? We met at the library. You gave me your –

JOHN DODGE. I remember. Sure. Hi. *(still looking around)* I think I bought something and left it at the store. That wasn't a very smart investment.

MRS. SWANSON. I've done that – it's so stupid. Hey, are you hungry? *(She sits down on a bench.)* I have some little sandwiches. I'm really hungry.

JOHN DODGE. That'd be great. *(still thinking about whatever he lost)* Damn it. *(brief pause)* I'm sorry – I would love a sandwich. *(He sits.)* Thanks.

MRS. SWANSON. Was that a tour going on?

JOHN DODGE. I'm sure it was something.

MRS. SWANSON. Here. *(She hands him a sandwich.)*

JOHN DODGE. Wow. They are little.

MRS. SWANSON. I have more.

JOHN DODGE. No, they're great, thanks. *(brief pause)* God, I had the worst night. Almost non-stop meaningful silence. Worst morning, too. Don't get married, that's my advice.

MRS. SWANSON. I'm already married.

JOHN DODGE. Oh, that's right, I forgot. Well, I hope you brought a good book.

MRS. SWANSON. I didn't know you're… Are you married?

JOHN DODGE. I was. All I remember is lying in bed, listening to the breathing. That's not true. We had some pretty good times. Probably my best. Yeah.

MRS. SWANSON. I'm sorry.

JOHN DODGE. It's sad. You sit around reading the side of a cereal box. Half the dishes are gone, half the cups, you eat everything out of a dented can, no more pretty shoes by the door, and, that's your little half-life. *(brief pause)* Definitely don't get divorced. I know, I'm all over the place on that one. *(brief pause)* Sorry. Are you getting settled here?

MRS. SWANSON. I am. We are. More and more. This is all a big change.

JOHN DODGE. What?

MRS. SWANSON. Here. And the whole idea of children.

JOHN DODGE. It is. I have two nieces.

MRS. SWANSON. Oh, how great – girls.

JOHN DODGE. They are great. You know what – it's just one niece, I think. The other one is her friend. I'm a terrible uncle. But, I don't know, I still feel like a nephew. Time, you know. "Buzzzzzzz." "Plink."

MRS. SWANSON. You said that the day we met.

JOHN DODGE. Something like it, I'm sure. It's a theory of mine.

MRS. SWANSON. It's not really a theory. You're just making different sounds with your mouth.

JOHN DODGE. So are you.

MRS. SWANSON. True. "True." *(brief pause)* How's gravity?

JOHN DODGE. It's all right, I guess. *(brief pause)* What?

MRS. SWANSON. You were reading a book about gravity.

JOHN DODGE. Oh, right. That's over. I just kind of lost the… you know. I mean, do I really need to know about that? Anyway, now, I'm taking this course on watercolor painting.

MRS. SWANSON. You're quite a Renaissance man.

JOHN DODGE. It's not really a course. It's just the directions that came with the paints.

MRS. SWANSON. Well, still, it sounds great.

JOHN DODGE. It's not. It's just some other thing.

MRS. SWANSON. I would think you'd make a really good uncle.

JOHN DODGE. I would too, but, yeah, no. I panic. Who wants a panicky uncle? I get anxious, you know?

MRS. SWANSON. I feel that way sometimes.

JOHN DODGE. Me too.

MRS. SWANSON. *(brief pause)* So, Bob is finishing up some things with work and our old house. He just started up in a new position. He should be here soon. I still don't really know the place. It can get lonely, can't it.

JOHN DODGE. Yeah. You get the mail, it's a clothes catalog. Maybe you leaf through it, maybe think, "Hey, I could buy those pants." Then you think, "But then it'd just be me, again, in a different pair of pants." Then you go out and walk around, and that's your day, time for bed.

MRS. SWANSON. That's kind of gloomy. I like looking at catalogs. Things aren't so bad. I visit Bob here and there, if he's at a convention or something nearby. He's in sales.

JOHN DODGE. I always wanted to be in something.

MRS. SWANSON. Yeah? Well, I'm sure you'll, you know....

JOHN DODGE. Yeah? That's nice. Thanks.

MRS. SWANSON. *(brief pause)* I've been having trouble sleeping.

JOHN DODGE. Oh, God – nighttime. Daytime, too. I'm like, "Enough – I get it." *(brief pause)* I read articles about identity theft and I actually get a little jealous, you know? "Just take it," you know. "Good luck, fella." Sometimes, I think I should just go quietly retire, you know, alone in the bathroom, with an X-acto knife. But then I start up some dumb project or get a book about some idiot thing.

MRS. SWANSON. *(with real sympathy)* John.

JOHN DODGE. You have a nice voice, um... I'm sorry...

MRS. SWANSON. Mary.

JOHN DODGE. Mary, of course. I like it.

MRS. SWANSON. We all have our dark nights. We're probably never as alone as we think.

JOHN DODGE. Yeah, no. We hope. *(brief pause)* I heard what you said. It probably seemed like I didn't, but I did. I'm really sorry you can't sleep.

MRS. SWANSON. Me too. No, thank you. *(moved, by even this very small kindness)* I know you're just making different sounds with your mouth again, but, thanks.

JOHN DODGE. I haven't asked you a lot about yourself.

MRS. SWANSON. Is that... are you asking now?

JOHN DODGE. I don't know – I just suddenly tried to picture you not sleeping. Sometimes you get used to the words for things, and then you suddenly remember the things. And so I suddenly saw you, the real Mary, not a word, staring out a window, or crying or reading, whatever you do.

MRS. SWANSON. I do read, sometimes. Or, yeah, sometimes, cry. That's nice of you to – it's nice you would picture me. In tears, or reading. *(brief pause)* Night is hard, you know? It gets so quiet. I never know what I'm supposed to be listening to. *(brief pause)* But it does give me time to catch up on my needless worry.

JOHN DODGE. *(small laugh)* I do that – what you just did.

MRS. SWANSON. What?

JOHN DODGE. Use humor to try to distance myself from the pain.

MRS. SWANSON. I was using humor to try to be funny.

JOHN DODGE. Yeah, that's something different. *(brief pause)* If you ever need any help, I'm pretty good with the needless worry.

MRS. SWANSON. The other night, I couldn't stop thinking, "What if my taste buds stop working?"

JOHN DODGE. Massive heart failure in a public place.

MRS. SWANSON. You can do better than that. Plus, that's really more of a guy thing.

JOHN DODGE. Cancer, in the privacy of your own home.

MRS. SWANSON. The old standby. And, yes, good — something for the ladies.

JOHN DODGE. *(without having laughed)* It's good to laugh. *(brief pause)* I like that thing you said — "dark nights."

MRS. SWANSON. I guess all nights are dark, but you know what I mean. *(brief pause)* Oh, I almost forgot. I'm hoping you can come have a look at something.

JOHN DODGE. I'd love to. What?

MRS. SWANSON. A plumbing thing. I think it's just a clogged drain.

JOHN DODGE. I was thinking maybe it was a painting or a sunset or something.

MRS. SWANSON. No. *(small smile)* Sorry.

JOHN DODGE. Yeah, I'll take a look. I could use the work. Not that I'd charge you. *(He gets up.)* Speaking of not making any money, I should get going. Hey, what's today?

MRS. SWANSON. Tuesday. *(or whatever the actual day is)*

JOHN DODGE. Oh, shit. I thought it was Monday. *(or whatever the actual day before would be)*

MRS. SWANSON. Sorry, again.

JOHN DODGE. I probably would have found out eventually.

MRS. SWANSON. I'll give you a call. Bye, John.

JOHN DODGE. Bye, Mary. It was really nice talking.

MRS. SWANSON. It was. Thank you. We should — yes. Definitely. Bye, see you later.

JOHN DODGE. Bye.

(He exits.)

(She begins to exit, then sits back down, lights fade.)

Scene Six

(Lights suggest evening. LIBRARIAN, *with her purse and some books, enters.)*

LIBRARIAN. *(to audience:)* That book came back today. I was just reading. Here: *(She reads, periodically clarifying terms for the audience.)* "Life had gone on. Several moons had passed." *(clarifying)* Several months. *(She reads.)* "The medicine man" – a medicine man is a doctor – "The medicine man shook his feathers. The villagers stood, shivering. A star shone over Inpetway." That's here. It was. *(She reads.)* "The medicine man spoke in difficult ways of difficult things, in the worried vocabulary of medicine and night. The villagers listened quietly, and quietly misunderstood. The sick man listened, and quietly got worse." For "sick man," just think of anybody, an average person. A child has written in the margin here: "anxiety, sickness, death, spiritual." *(She quickly shows us.)* She writes in these wonderful loopy letters in a bright red pen. At least, I think it's a girl. *(She reads.)* "The medicine man continued – differently, now. His calm eyes sparkled slowly, as he turned to the blushing woman there." The "blushing woman" is probably a bride or a woman falling in love. *(She reads.)* "He spoke now in simple ways of simple things. He asked the moon to be beautiful. He asked the sun to come to warm the unborn child and the born mother. He asked the people to be human and the animals to stay animals. He asked the Universe to expand. He said, deeply, to all of them, "Great things. Oh, Great things. Someone is born, someone will die, both are you. Unwind, unknow." The same little girl has written a question mark, here. *(brief pause)* I read once the question mark comes from a musical notation used in Gregorian Chants, to signal that the phrase should have an upward intonation, that it should rise upward, to heaven. Imagine this little red one here – no sentence, no question, just a little red question mark, by itself – rising up to heaven, to God. Imagine the look on His face. *(leafing forward a few pages)* Later, she's written the word "atmosphere." And here's a barrette she used for a book mark. Ah, literature. *(Brief pause. Looking up:)* It's a beautiful night. Whether or not there's anything up there.

Scene Seven

(GREG is in a space capsule, floating. The following lines are amplified, with some static and perhaps some delay, as though a radio transmission. Both GREG and GROUND CONTROL are mainly pre-occupied with computer figures and flight adjustments and are not really interested in poetry or philosophy, though these things seem to arise, driven by the circumstance of being in space and seeing Earth. GROUND CONTROL may be seated on stage, perhaps facing away from the audience.)

GROUND CONTROL. Cormorant Nine. *(pause)* Cormorant Nine. This is Ground Control, Houston. Do you read? Do you copy?

GREG. This is C-9. Copy. Sounds like you're in my living room. Over.

GROUND CONTROL. The things we can do. Go ahead, C-9. How's life?

GREG. What a view, is one thing. I've heard about it. But, what a wonderful… I never knew how round round was, Houston. God. All this space, it's just pure majesty, it's endless, majestic. But it's cold, it's almost just raw data, raw mathematics. Then you see little planet Earth and – my God, she's just so welcoming and good. Seems like a symphony should be playing. It, wow, it's just this beautiful fragile thing, something a happy child would draw. It's so blue. Houston.

GROUND CONTROL. *(Indistinct sentence. Something like, "Fivv – . Gull sensor. Ooh min. Ive.")*

GREG. Repeat, please.

GROUND CONTROL. Fifty-one degrees. Angle sensor arm, two minutes forty-five.

GREG. Copy. Arm is in position. *(A short indistinct sentence.)*

GROUND CONTROL. What's that? Didn't catch that.

GREG. *(pause)* Sorry?

GROUND CONTROL. Go ahead, Greg.

GREG. Oh. I'm just trying to picture life, back home. There's a guy there I remember, thought he found a meteorite, once. It was normal sedimentary rock, just made from dead animals and plants crushed together. He was disappointed. Shouldn't have been. I was never crazy about him, I think he bashed my mailbox in, but, he shouldn't have been sad. That rock, that guy who found it, the field he found it in, all these things are miraculous because all these things are earthly. The words he used to refer to it, the breath it took to make the words, all of it. Just sacredly and profoundly and mysteriously – well, yeah – earthly.

GROUND CONTROL. Are you getting mystical on us, Greg?

GREG. I'm just looking and talking, Houston. I didn't prepare anything.

GROUND CONTROL. Just giving you a hard time, partner.

GREG. Okay.

GROUND CONTROL. Looking good. Go ahead.

GREG. I'm done. But I just have to say, it doesn't look lonely from up here. Everything looks right-next-door. It's where you're sitting, right now. How 'bout that. You're breathing the Earth's atmosphere. You got mountains and clouds, oceans. People out doing things together. Soccer games and birthday parties, listening to beautiful music. Inexpressible, you know. How'd we get so lucky? *(brief pause)* I probably sound like a real cliché. Me, with my chiseled features and the flight suit, waxing all poetic. Waxing all fragile and religious.

GROUND CONTROL. All right, Greg. *(brief pause)* Synchronize, one seven six.

GREG. Synchronize.

GROUND CONTROL. Copy. *(Pause. An eerie sound.)* Say again, Cormorant Niner?

GREG. I didn't say anything. Go ahead, Houston.

GROUND CONTROL. Roger. No matter. Looking good. We do recommend P65 alignment, plus point two two.

GREG. Thank you – P65, plus point two two. *(brief pause)* I'm looking out at the world. I'm thinking about people. I can't tell you what this is like. Over.

GROUND CONTROL. Copy.

GREG. Maybe everybody knows what this is like.

GROUND CONTROL. Maybe they do. Wunderbar, Greg. Looking good. We have no abnormalities. Over.

GREG. Roger. Oxygen is good.

GROUND CONTROL. It sure is. All right, partner. Come home soon.

(Static. Static fades.)

Scene Eight

(The SWANSON's *kitchen.* JOHN DODGE *is working on the kitchen-sink drain. He is lying on the floor, periodically ducking in and out of the cabinet, and therefore periodically inaudible. At the top of the scene,* JOHN DODGE *is on his back, his head and upper torso hidden in the cabinet.* MRS. SWANSON *is at the kitchen counter.)*

MRS. SWANSON. Seriously, John, thanks for helping out. Bob and I are grateful.

JOHN DODGE. *(appears from under the sink to grab a wrench)* No, it's no trouble. When does he get here?

MRS. SWANSON. Any day, I hope. It's crazy. We used to just be regular people. We said "good night" and "good morning," every day. All of a sudden we're so modern. It's funny. *(brief pause)* Have you always done this kind of work?

JOHN DODGE. God, yeah. In fact, I've been thinking about that philosophy thing about how you can't step in the same river twice. It turns out you can. Sometimes, I feel like I should just... I don't know. I try, you know, but some days it all just seems like the...

(Disappears under the sink. Indecipherable end to the sentence.)

MRS. SWANSON. *(enthusiastically agreeing:)* I know. I know what you mean. Everything suddenly looks like it's spelled wrong, or something. Like, even your own name looks like a typo.

JOHN DODGE. Yeah, exactly. I'm always getting, I don't know, I told you this, I get these awful panic attacks. They're actually how I stay in shape. It's a mess. Enough about me, and how I sometimes get claustrophobia and can't swim.

(Indistinct short question: a muffled and indecipherable version of "So how does it feel being pregnant?")

MRS. SWANSON. What?

JOHN DODGE. *(Repeated, mainly as before.)*

MRS. SWANSON. Oh. It's so new. I don't think I could even describe it. I'm really excited. But it's almost like it's just words, at this point.

JOHN DODGE. *(Indistinct medium-length sentence. A muffled and indecipherable version of "It's probably just words at every point.")*

MRS. SWANSON. You're probably right – it's just words at every point. It scares me, though. Having a baby. The words seem so tiny and quiet, compared to the truth of it. Compared with if you really try to picture it. Not to mention, just, the whole thing. I mean, do I look like the kind of person?

JOHN DODGE. *(Indistinct sentence, muffled and indecipherable version of "I think you're quite intoxicating.")*

MRS. SWANSON. Well, thank you, John. I don't think I've ever been called "intoxicating" before. That's very flattering.

JOHN DODGE. *(appears)* I hope you don't think of me as just some kind of a... I don't know. Because I have so much going on inside me. A lot of different... *(brief pause)* You know, people laughed when I said I wanted to get a law degree.

MRS. SWANSON. You have a law degree?

JOHN DODGE. Me? Oh God no. People really laughed, though. *(brief pause)* I've wanted a lot, out of life. First, air and milk, and then it just kept going.

MRS. SWANSON. Well, you've gotten a lot, too, haven't you? In life?

JOHN DODGE. I had shingles, once. I'm kidding. Well, no, I'm not, actually – I did have that. Good argument for death, by the way – shingles. Nice reminder your skin's an enemy.

MRS. SWANSON. Your skin's probably your best friend.

JOHN DODGE. For a while, sure. *(very brief pause)* I have a kind of serious mind/body problem. But, I know what you're saying. I try to be grateful for what I have.

MRS. SWANSON. I wish I had more gratitude. When you think of all the miracles it takes just to sit in a chair. A billion things going right, just to sit here. And do nothing. And watch you work. Miracles.

JOHN DODGE. You get used to them, though. That's the sad thing. You look around: miracle, miracle, miracle. It's tiring. It's sad. Or scary. *(indistinct short sentence)*

MRS. SWANSON. That's kind of extreme, isn't it? But, I guess, to be completely honest, it's always an option.

JOHN DODGE. *(Indistinct short sentence. A muffled and indecipherable version of: "Except for the fact that I'm afraid of dying.")*

MRS. SWANSON. *(laughing)* You can say that again. Oh, Johnny Boy, you can say that again.

(JOHN DODGE, *appearing from under the sink*)

JOHN DODGE. That I'm afraid of dying?

MRS. SWANSON. I thought you said something different.

JOHN DODGE. No.

(He removes a handful of sludge from the drain, puts it onto a piece of newspaper.)

There.

MRS. SWANSON. Yuck. Is that the problem?

JOHN DODGE. Yeah.

MRS. SWANSON. What is it?

JOHN DODGE. Just years of stuff. Sort of a metaphor for – yeah, no, just years of stuff, gunk.

(He stands up, and is slightly disoriented.)

Whoa. I stood up too quick. My whole life, I don't think I ever stood up at the right speed. All life long, John Dodge in the wrong. "All life long," wow, that's hard to say.

MRS. SWANSON. No it isn't.

JOHN DODGE. *(effortlessly)* "All life long." No, you're right – it isn't. I think I better sit down for a few seconds. *(He sits down.)* One one-thousand, two one-thousand, three one-thousand. Okay. *(He stands up, same disorientation.)* Wow. Did it again.

*(**MRS. SWANSON** takes his hand.)*

MRS. SWANSON. Maybe you're just a dizzy person. They say some people have trouble with the Earth's, you know, with the rotation.

JOHN DODGE. Yeah, maybe that's – yeah.

MRS. SWANSON. *(brief pause)* John.

JOHN DODGE. Again, she says, in her nice voice, "John."

MRS. SWANSON. *(small slightly nervous laugh)* Well, what am I supposed to say? *(brief pause)* Are you all right?

(She lets his hand go. Very brief pause.)

We haven't known each other very long, but, do I seem different?

JOHN DODGE. How?

MRS. SWANSON. I don't know. Somehow. Inside.

JOHN DODGE. Yeah, I don't know. Kind of. Yeah, you do.

MRS. SWANSON. *(small smile)* Good.

JOHN DODGE. Change.

MRS. SWANSON. I know.

JOHN DODGE. You smiled when you said "Good." That says a lot about you. You look really well. I bet you'll be a radiant mother. *(pause)* I don't have anything, Mary. Sorry, big change of topic, but – I don't. Look at me. I have a bunch of hobbies I quit and some overdue books I never read. I don't have anything.

MRS. SWANSON. Yes, you do. Come on. Yes, you do.

JOHN DODGE. Mary, I don't.

MRS. SWANSON. Maybe you're not looking hard enough.

JOHN DODGE. *(Pause. Short indistinct sentence, somewhat clearly vocalized.)* Mome gavnerma thurn.

MRS. SWANSON. What?

JOHN DODGE. Just joking, because of the – *(He points to the cabinet.)* Remember when you couldn't hear me?

MRS. SWANSON. Oh, right. *(She covers her mouth and says an indistinct line, about five syllables long, perhaps something like "Gabralldee yo fon gerg fonderall.")*

JOHN DODGE. Hmm. I never thought of it that way.

(They share a little laugh. Brief pause.)

Mary, I'm looking as hard as I can.

(Lights down.)

Scene Nine

(COP enters darkened stage with powerful flashlight. Perhaps he comes into the audience. Behind him, intermission audience enters unnoticeably and is seated, facing actual audience.)

(He shines the light into the face of an actual audience member. Moves the light to another audience member, and then another.)

COP. Don't worry. People always look so worried. *(shines light around the stage)* We got a report of some problem, down here. Some trouble. A scream, maybe a loud sigh, a couple of sighs, something. I'm sure it's fine. Just normal people being human in the night. Inner life meeting outer life. Bang. Kapow. But, yeah. Nothing to worry about.

(He shines the light back over the stage.)

Sleep tight, pretty Middletown. All is well.

(Flashlight goes out. COP bangs it on his leg a couple of times. It comes back on.)

There we go. Okay. Pray the Lord your soul to keep. Something like that. Whatever makes you feel calm. *(very brief pause)* Just be all right.

(He exits.)

Scene Ten

(The intermission of this play. Lights that suggest house-lighting come up. Recorded applause. The intermission audience, seated on stage, applauds.)

(Intermission audience is made up of **FREELANCER,** **MAN** *and* **WOMAN** *(on a date),* **SWEETHEART** *(a girl with a mild mental disability) and her* **AUNT.** *Some have programs for "MIDDLETOWN." Almost all of* **SWEETHEART**'s *lines are said very loudly, but not shouted.* **FREELANCER** *is writing in a notebook.)*

AUNT. *(brief pause)* I should have brought a sweater. Are you cold, sweetheart?

SWEETHEART. Feelings.

AUNT. Remember, we're inside. *(to others:)* Excuse me. *(to* **SWEETHEART***:)* Would you like some candy?

SWEETHEART. "What about when English dies."

AUNT. Nice and quiet, dear.

(gives **SWEETHEART** *some candy)*

FREELANCER. That's from the play. *(He writes.)*

MAN. *(standing and stretching)* Excuse me. *(He exits.)*

AUNT. *(to* **FREELANCER***:)* You're very busy.

FREELANCER. I'm writing a book on being an audience member. Originally, I wanted to be an autobiographer.

AUNT. Oh?

FREELANCER. Yeah. But then I had to sit down and ask myself, "Seriously? Me?"

AUNT. What do you like to go see?

FREELANCER. Oh, God, anything and everything. I've seen horses being born, Egyptian tombs being exhumed. I've gone whale watching, I watched my poor mother die, saw a Hindu bathing festival, a total solar eclipse, you name it. Mainly plays. Sometimes, I have anxiety attacks when the curtain goes up.

WOMAN. I always want to cry at the end. When you see the actors smiling and bowing in the light. Dead kings waving to their wives and girlfriends.

SWEETHEART. "Be a good human."

FREELANCER. That was in there, too, right at the beginning. I have the worst memory. But I like to write down lines. *(As he writes down the line. To* AUNT*:)* Your daughter has an amazing memory.

AUNT. She certainly does. She's my niece.

FREELANCER. Well, she has a very good memory. *(to* SWEETHEART*:)* What's your first memory, ever?

(Long pause. No response from SWEETHEART*.)*

It's hard, isn't it. *(brief pause)* I was always sitting somewhere. I was born in the audience.

AUNT. I like when plays have a break in the middle. Once, we met an oceanography student. *(to* SWEETHEART*:)* Remember, he painted the garage? It's nice.

FREELANCER. It's funny, though. Since you don't know the end, you're not sure what you're in the middle of. Hey. *(Pleased with the thought, he writes it down.)*

*(*MAN *enters.)*

MAN. Much better. Are we talking about the play? Let me ask, so the town is like a –

AUNT. *(interrupting:)* The town is called Middletown. But it has other names.

MAN. Yeah, I got that. But the people are –

AUNT. *(interrupting:)* I think the main two are having a romance. They represent the future, I think.

MAN. Thanks. I really enjoyed that.

WOMAN. I had a neighbor like the John guy. If you talked to him, he would listen so hard, but you weren't sure what he was listening to. He finally left or something bad happened. It was really sad. He didn't have anybody. At least, the guy in the play has the lady who just moved in.

AUNT. Mary.

SWEETHEART. "Houston."

AUNT. *(to* SWEETHEART*:)* Houston is in Texas.

SWEETHEART. "Your daughter has an amazing memory."

FREELANCER. *(standing, stretching)* My back is killing me. I think it's growing into the shape of a chair.

SWEETHEART. "I have the worst memory."

WOMAN. *(brief pause)* You know what's funny? So, everything, in a way, is still going on. Time's going by, in the town, at the library, in outer space, here – all over. In a fictional way, of course, but, at the same time, like, non-fictionally, too.

MAN. Relativity.

WOMAN. *(brief pause)* Is that your contribution?

MAN. Yeah. Just, everything's all… I don't know – Sir Albert Einstein.

WOMAN. I don't think he was ever knighted, but, okay. *(to* AUNT *and* FREELANCER*:)* But, do you know what I'm saying? Something's coming.

AUNT. But we don't know what.

WOMAN. Neither do they. They're right in the middle of some life in some town – you know, in a way.

AUNT. They deserve something good. We all do.

SWEETHEART. "Life."

AUNT. It's quite a topic, isn't it. I think she's pregnant, Mrs. Swenson. There's always a glow, a kind of shadow. You can tell.

FREELANCER. It's always a possibility.

MAN. So is suicide.

WOMAN. Where did that come from?

MAN. I don't know, my mouth? Where does anything come from? Where do crocodiles come from?

FREELANCER. Dinosaurs. But where do dinosaurs come from? And so on, down the ages. Until we're asking, "Where did nothing come from?" King Lear has an answer. King James has another.

MAN. I was just floating it out there. I don't know – somebody said "possibilities." *(Brief pause. Shaking his foot.)* Man, my foot is totally asleep. It must be bored.

FREELANCER. This one culture whose name I forget thought the soul resided in the feet. Other peoples have located it in the hands, or the eyes, the heart, all over the whole body.

SWEETHEART. "Peoples."

WOMAN. *(to SWEETHEART:)* Yeah. *(brief pause)* It's funny. The Soul. The Afterlife. We say words like that like we say words like Shoe and February. But, just honestly, just imagine, for one second.

MAN. It changes things. Life.

WOMAN. Mm hmm. *(to FREELANCER:)* And it's like the thing you said. You don't know what the end is, so how can you know what you're in the middle of? They don't know what happens to you when you die, so how can they know, really, what happens to you when you're born?

FREELANCER. A serious mystery, then the middle part, then another mystery. That's pretty good. *(He gestures that he'd like to write this down. To WOMAN:)* May I?

WOMAN. Please.

(FREELANCER writes.)

MAN. Hey, so, where's the husband, anyway? Is he supposed to represent something?

AUNT. Just a regular human being, I think. Maybe they have weekends together. People always figure something out. We're always scurrying around, looking over our shoulders, figuring something out. People. *(brief pause)* We saw a play once that had an angel in it. A school production or some kind of community thing. Remember?

SWEETHEART. "Just a regular human being, I think."

WOMAN. *(to SWEETHEART:)* You get everything word for word. It's a real gift. *(no response)*

FREELANCER. It's strange, though. It's like a museum exhibit about the last ten minutes. But it is – you're right, she's incredible. What a thing. Language, you know. Repeatability. Time, grammar, us. Weird.

WOMAN. Is, Was, Will be.

FREELANCER. That pretty much covers it. *(brief pause)* I've been all over the world.

AUNT. *(musingly)* "Is, Was, Will be."

WOMAN. *(nodding)* Story of my life.

FREELANCER. I've seen so many things. Huh.

MAN. *(having noticed the armrest of his chair is loose)* Look at this. *(He holds up the detached part.)* This just comes completely off. *(He reattaches it.)*

FREELANCER. All that travel, all the cathedrals and wonderful meals and evening light and people dying, and what are my findings? What's my conclusion? "Huh."

AUNT. *(looking in her purse)* Usually I'll pack a little something to eat.

SWEETHEART. "Huh."

FREELANCER. Yeah. Exactly.

SWEETHEART. "People always look so worried."

FREELANCER. They do. Right. The cop said that.

SWEETHEART. People know what happens.

FREELANCER. *(wondering whom SWEETHEART is quoting:)* Who said that?

AUNT. *(leafing through her program)* People are born, people die. *(patting* SWEETHEART *on the knee)* We'll go to that nice place you like, after. We can do the treasure map on the placemat. I always loved those.

(The lights on the intermission audience dim three times, signaling the intermission is ended.)

And here we go. Exciting.

(Lights down as house lights come up.)

End of Act One

(Intermission)

ACT TWO

(Months later. Middletown.)

Scene One

*(**MECHANIC** enters the dimly-lit stage, from the opposite direction that **COP** came from in Scene One, and comes to the window of **JOHN DODGE**'s house, in which we see **JOHN DODGE**, illuminated, staring out intently. He cleans a piece of lint off the glass with his finger, revealing that he was just staring at the pane of glass. **MECHANIC** crouches nearby.)*

MECHANIC. *(He imitates the sound of a crow.)* Ca-caa. Ca-caa.

*(**JOHN DODGE** barely reacts, except to shake his head in a very small way, as if quietly but deeply pained by the sound, and then moves from the window. **MECHANIC** moves across stage, to where **MRS. SWANSON**, visible in her window, is looking at herself in a mirror. She is very pregnant. **MECHANIC** makes a heavy long breathing sound.)*

Hhhhaaahh. Hhhhaaahh. *(crow sound, again)* Ca-caa.

*(**MRS. SWANSON** moves toward the window, looking frightened. **MECHANIC** hides.)*

MRS. SWANSON. *(muffled:)* Is someone there? *(She moves from the window.)*

MECHANIC. *(He steps out of his hiding place. To audience:)* Just some regular sounds from nature. Probably nothing to be too afraid of. *(He makes a few long whooshing sounds like the ocean or the wind in the trees.)* Whhhshhhhhhh. Whhhshhhhhhh. That's my impression of a cell dividing – or, I don't know, metastasizing. Same thing, probably, for a while – until it isn't. I learned that word through relatives. *(brief pause)* By the way, I started drinking, again. I don't know if people know that I'd stopped for a while? I did. Everything was better. But I decided to start up again. You might be asking yourselves: "Why?"

(Brief pause. He stays still and looks through the audience, suspiciously, but also with a kind of open curiosity.)

That was a little chance to let your minds wander, to let you come up with some reasons for me.

(Another pause, same as above.)

That was some time just for you.

*(**MECHANIC** takes a sip from a bottle.)*

Away!

(Brief pause. He slowly exits.)

Scene Two

(Entrance and lawn of Middletown Hospital. Bright day. A sign that says "Emergency" is staked into the grass. LANDSCAPER is on his knees on the grass, preparing to plant a tree, a young sapling. COP enters and quietly approaches LANDSCAPER from behind. COP holds his hand out in the shape of gun, aimed at the back of LANDSCAPER's head.)

COP. Bang!

LANDSCAPER. *(Startled. Recovers.)* Jesus. Hey.

COP. I could have killed you, just then.

LANDSCAPER. And that's somehow my fault?

COP. Planting a tree?

LANDSCAPER. Great work – you solved the case of what I'm doing.

COP. Don't be smart.

LANDSCAPER. Done.

COP. How's my sister?

LANDSCAPER. She's good. She wants you to come over for dinner, next week. We finished the new patio and we're having a cookout. *(some business with the tree)*

COP. Sounds good. *(very brief pause)* What type is it? Elm?

LANDSCAPER. White Ash, I think. Although it could be a Green Ash. They're surprisingly hard to tell apart.

COP. Fair enough. *(brief pause)* Pretty day.

LANDSCAPER. *(looking for a place to plant the tree)* Where do you think this should go?

COP. I don't know – somewhere. *(Brief pause. Shaking his head, contemplatively, somewhat disdainfully:)* People.

LANDSCAPER. I know. *(brief pause)* Actually, I don't know. What, specifically, about people?

COP. Just: people. The things they do. You think you know people. You don't. You think you caught some non-suicidal gleam in their eye. You didn't. You never know what people are going to do.

(On the COP *'s lines above,* LANDSCAPER *picks a spot on the grass, stands straight and still. Immediately after the* COP *has finished speaking,* LANDSCAPER *gently sways for a few moments, his eyes closed, pretending he's a tree, making the sound of wind in the leaves.)*

LANDSCAPER. Whhhshhhhhhh. Whhhshhhhhhh. This feels good, right here. What do you think about here?

COP. I'm sure that'll be fine. Ninety-nine percent of the trees on earth weren't planted by anybody.

LANDSCAPER. *(digging, preparing)* So they wheeled some guy past here, this morning. He lifted his head up, you know, "Wait, wait, one more look." That was a sight. Then a pregnant lady went in, crying, trying to carry all her stuff. She looked so lonely, which, you know, when you think about it, she totally isn't. It made me wish the thing was already done. I think it'll be soothing, you know, this tree, just nice for people. Bald kids going in on sunny school days. Shattered families leaving in the rain. Just a good old tree. Year in, year out.

COP. Sure.

LANDSCAPER. Maybe someday some young lovers'll carve their initials into it.

(He pinches the tree, not even an inch in diameter, with thumb and forefinger.)

Into this. Pretty incomprehensible: The future.

COP. There are some guidelines, some givens.

LANDSCAPER. Yeah, maybe. *(He begins to dig.)* I buried some sunglasses around back, this morning. Just to give somebody something to find, someday. *(He strikes something with the shovel.)* Hey, what's that? *(picks up the object, which is a rock)* I always think it's going to be gold or a skull or something. *(Brief pause. Holding up the rock.)* Alas. That's got to be a really old word: "Rock." *(He carefully sets the rock aside.)*

COP. It fits pretty well, doesn't it.

LANDSCAPER. It sounds like a name the rocks would've picked out themselves. Same thing with Tree.

(He digs up another small rock and places it on top of the other and looks at the two rocks.)

There. A monument to the moment of its own construction.

COP. A rock a person put on top of another rock.

LANDSCAPER. There's that word again. It's got a real honest ring to it: "rock." "Person," on the other hand – I'm not so sure. It feels sort of last-minute, doesn't it? Sort of fleeting? "Person."

COP. Sounds like an average-paying job.

LANDSCAPER. It does. "I'm a person. Been one for years, now. It's okay. The benefits, and so on. Of course, I'm not going to do it forever."

COP. This isn't really my kind of conversation.

LANDSCAPER. No?

COP. Yeah, not really. In fact, I've got to go in here. It's potentially a crime scene, if you can believe it. Tell my sister I said hi. I'll see you later.

*(**COP** exits, to enter the hospital.)*

LANDSCAPER. See you later, person. I mean that in all the best ways.

(He digs up another rock, and places it on top of the others, making a tiny snowman or a semi-human statue.)

Rock. Tree. *(He pokes in the dirt.)* Worm.

(Stands up straight, leans on his shovel and sighs.)

Scene Three

(MALE DOCTOR's office. MRS. SWANSON and MALE DOCTOR. MRS. SWANSON is very pregnant. MALE DOCTOR, though entirely compassionate, is also very busy, and he speaks quickly. He is periodically writing, filling out forms, and referring to notes throughout this scene.)

MALE DOCTOR. There's a problem – no, sorry, there's no problem. That's "Swenson." You're Swanson. Sorry. Now, we did some more tests on your little man. Everything looks very good. His Babinski Reflex, for example.

MRS. SWANSON. Is that where you –

MALE DOCTOR. *(interrupting, nodding)* Right – that's where we stroke the foot to see if the toes curl. We do this with sound and tiny beams of light. We can do almost all these tests prior to the actual birth, now. It's incredible. In a few more years, people won't even have to be born. Anyway, he was magnificent. The first expressive gesture. From that little curl of the toes to all of the world's bibles and languages, it's just a matter of time. Everybody watched on the monitor. You probably heard a cheer go up from the other room. It's like a space launch. Long way away, but, he could be a tiny little Beethoven, your boy. Get him a fun little drum or a bell. Now, will the father be in the room with you?

MRS. SWANSON. He said he would, yes.

MALE DOCTOR. Good. It's good to have someone. This is literally going to be the first day of the rest of your baby's life. Linguistically, you'll want to start him out small. Simple words like hi and juice and tree and bye-bye. Say whatever you feel. Most of it happens on a vibrational level, anyway.

(A brief staticky buzz. A voice comes over the office intercom.)

INTERCOM. I'm sorry, Doctor – I have Mrs. Swenson on the line.

MALE DOCTOR. *(Brief pause. To* **INTERCOM***:)* Tell her I'm very sorry. I'll have to call her right back. *(to* **MRS. SWANSON***:)* Excuse me. That's a sad story. But, back to you. We'll generate a birth certificate, of course. That'll start up the paper trail. Do you have a name?

MRS. SWANSON. We're thinking possibly "John."

MALE DOCTOR. "John" is perfect. Biblical, one syllable, no complicated back-story, just "John." "John Swanson." It's like a little poem. *(very brief pause)* What else?

MRS. SWANSON. Can I ask you… sorry, this is so general, but… I mean, what should I do? How should I be?

MALE DOCTOR. Those are great questions. And here's my answer. Love is all. It sounds so simple, I know, but, give him love. Without it, he'll just go around the world saying different things and seeing this and that and none of it'll make any difference. You've seen the type. Out in the rain, just kind of rattling around in their bodies. But, it's easy. This is the time for smiles and simple rhymes. Let's see you smile.

*(***MRS. SWANSON*** smiles. He barely smiles.)*

Great. Wow. Did you see? You made me smile, too. Let's be honest, part of the whole great March of Humanity is just swinging your arms and walking, just smiling and moving forward. One other thing is: you never know. So be forgiving, of yourself, of him, of nature, everything. Nature is so insane, it's so rough, and we're just humans, just these chatty mammals with different names and colorful clothing. So, forgiveness, forgiveness and love, and you're all set. Now, I'm speaking quickly, and I'm sure there's a lot of huge gaps in my thinking. Apologies, I'm sorry, I make this speech a lot.

MRS. SWANSON. No, no, it's great, it sounds completely unrehearsed. Thank you. I'm grateful for anything. It's good to hear these things. *(She rubs her eye.)*

MALE DOCTOR. Does your eye itch?

MRS. SWANSON. A little. Is that a problem?

MALE DOCTOR. Just for you. Because it itches.

MRS. SWANSON. Oh, right. Is there anything else I should do? In the first little while?

MALE DOCTOR. Just hold him tight, hold the little human tight. Sing as much as you can. After the first few weeks, the amniotic fluid will drain from his ears. Before that, mercifully, everything is just a muffled kind of music. Same as in the womb. Right now, to him, most words probably sound a lot like the word "mother." Or "hearth" or "Earth," something indistinct like that, sort of rounded off. Who knows what shamanistic sense he's making of it all, you know? *(He speaks toward her belly.)* "Mahherhm. Herhomm. Mome gavnerma thurn." As far as he knows, the whole world is a soft little murmur of gentle intent. His instinct is going to be to trust life. His actual animal instinct – I never get over this – is to hold your hand. He's in there, right now, listening, forming, waiting to hold your hand. Wow, huh? Neither science nor religion has yet undone the wonder of the crying baby in air and light, grasping onto a finger.

MRS. SWANSON. You make it all sound so noble. Which it is, which I'm sure it is. *(brief pause)* I'm sort of alone, in this, at the moment. I'm sort of afraid, sometimes. It's hard to believe so many women have done this before.

MALE DOCTOR. Oh, but they did. And they were scared. And they did great. So be scared. Be yourself. You look great. You look like someone's mother. Don't forget – it's so easy to forget, but – everyone in the world was born. Try to name someone who wasn't. You can't. So just be a part of the whole crazy thing. The rest is details, little tests, taps of a tiny hammer. Oh, take one of these.

(He hands her a tiny white cotton hat.)

I get these free. Isn't it great? Did you ever see a tinier hat? Anyway, don't worry, why worry, come on, it's life. It's just good old life, been going on for years. *(brief pause)* It's a lot, all at once, isn't it.

MRS. SWANSON. Well, it's just all sort of surreal.

MALE DOCTOR. It is. But it's also sort of real. But, you're right, it's strange. A little person inside you is going to come out of you.

MRS. SWANSON. It's almost vaudevillian.

MALE DOCTOR. It is, yes. *(He doesn't laugh.)* That's very funny. But let's not overthink it. This is one time it makes good sense to just sit back and breathe and try to believe in miracles.

MRS. SWANSON. All right, I will. *(brief pause)* What happens to you when you're born? *(very brief pause)* Does it hurt?

MALE DOCTOR. Okay. Distress is certainly the first event. I'm sure there's a lot of pain, maybe even infinite pain, seeing as all we've known before has been infinite warmth. Even the gentlest birth must feel like a car crash. We'll probably never know the full effect. It could be the full effect is our life, our personality. Then it's over. He'll fall asleep in your arms, on your chest. He'll grasp your finger, because that's what the deepest thing in him tells him to do. It's so beautiful, it's so mysterious. You won't believe it. We have three.

MRS. SWANSON. Congratulations. That must be great.

MALE DOCTOR. It is. They are. My wife – her name is Jen – she said she forgot the pain, the worry, everything, the second she saw our firstborn. And she suddenly understood this word she'd been hearing all her life – Love. I felt it, too. You can't really describe it. As for the actual birth, we were worried, too, but, no surprises.

MRS. SWANSON. I'm glad. *(brief pause)* What about yours?

MALE DOCTOR. What, my own birth? Oh. I don't know. I'm sure it was fine.

MRS. SWANSON. Were you close to your mother?

MALE DOCTOR. I don't know, yeah, you know – just regular mother and son. She's still with us. Great lady. *(very brief pause)* What else, anything else?

MRS. SWANSON. I'm sure, but nothing I can think of.

MALE DOCTOR. I see you brought some stay-over things. Good. You're going to be great. Now, I'm sorry, please, excuse me. I really have to return this phone call. Go take a stroll. Walking is good. It's what we do. We hold hands and we walk. Activity can help the labor along. All right?

MRS. SWANSON. Thank you. Yes. Thanks.

MALE DOCTOR. Good. Perfect. Sorry I have to rush.

MRS. SWANSON. No, I appreciate your time. If I think of anything or if I have any – you're busy, sorry, thanks. Bye.

MALE DOCTOR. Great. Sorry. See you soon.

(**MRS. SWANSON** *exits.* **MALE DOCTOR** *begins looking through some paperwork.*)

Now, Swenson, Swenson… Swenson or Swanson?

(Quickly checks some other paperwork.)

Swenson. One vowel away. Ahhhh. Eeee. Owww.

Scene Four

(Hospital room. **JOHN DODGE** *is in bed.)*

*(***FEMALE DOCTOR** *enters. Checks chart at the foot of the bed, etc.)*

FEMALE DOCTOR. How are you feeling?

JOHN DODGE. *(quietly)* Okay, I think.

FEMALE DOCTOR. Good. *(brief pause)* Sorry. This is difficult.

JOHN DODGE. I know. *(brief pause)* What is?

FEMALE DOCTOR. Well, we don't know each other. Of course. So it's hard to know how to begin.

JOHN DODGE. *(pause)* Are you going to try? *(brief pause)* I know what you're thinking. I'm not this kind of person.

FEMALE DOCTOR. What kind of person?

JOHN DODGE. I'm normally just a face in the crowd. In fact, I'm normally just home, by myself. Just a face in my house. Which is fine, normally. I don't think that – I don't know.

FEMALE DOCTOR. Go ahead, what were you going to say?

JOHN DODGE. Maybe I'm imbalanced. Or, I was. But I don't think I'm suicidal, deep-down. Even though, I mean, here I am, yes. And I think I'm probably making you feel uncomfortable.

FEMALE DOCTOR. I'm sure that's a little true. Thank you for your consideration. It's complicated.

JOHN DODGE. It is. I didn't know what I was doing. It was like this cloud came over me, this big dark idea.

FEMALE DOCTOR. And that was what?

JOHN DODGE. That I wanted to be an emergency, somehow. I always felt like one, deep-down. I've got all these weird problems. I get nervous in certain weather. Sunlight reminds me of this great woman I knew. My heart races, I get these twitches in my elbow, my mind races. *(brief pause)* It always scared me there was even a

word: Suicide. It scared me they even had a word for
it. And then, suddenly, there I am, you know, on my
kitchen floor, like a crazy person, right in the thick of
that word.

FEMALE DOCTOR. Forgive me, but, you used some kind of
a knife?

JOHN DODGE. A house-painting tool. Like, a scraper thing.

FEMALE DOCTOR. That sounds dirty.

JOHN DODGE. What do you mean?

FEMALE DOCTOR. That it might have had dirt on it. Germs.

JOHN DODGE. Maybe. Probably. *(brief pause)* I pictured
everybody with their eyes all red, saying funeral stuff
like, "We hardly knew him." And, in reality, they really
didn't. I never thought I'd have a lonely life. I do, it
turns out. Like, medically lonely. Like I've got sad
genes. Like, what's that word? *(very brief pause)* I don't
know. I'm sure there is one.

FEMALE DOCTOR. I'm sorry.

JOHN DODGE. Please don't worry. I know I'm not crazy. I'm
just sad. And not even that much, right now. I even
feel hungry. That must be a good sign. *(very brief pause)*
I keep explaining, but – I wanted to see if I had a
survival instinct. It was a stupid way to find out, but I
did. And I'm glad. And I'm better, I think. Not fine,
but, better.

FEMALE DOCTOR. That's the thing.

JOHN DODGE. It really is. *(brief pause)* What do you mean?

FEMALE DOCTOR. Well, we're not sure. Now, I just want to
take a look at this.

*(She puts on rubber gloves and pulls up the cotton mask
hanging around her neck. She gently opens the surgical
gauze covering the wound on his wrist.)*

JOHN DODGE. It smells really bad.

FEMALE DOCTOR. That's bacteria. It could just be topical.
But we're concerned. We're worried you might have
something serious.

JOHN DODGE. Me?

FEMALE DOCTOR. An infection. We want to be cautious.

JOHN DODGE. Okay. Is "we" you and me?

FEMALE DOCTOR. All of us here. We might need to do a biopsy. I'll have them dress this again.

(She gently replaces the bandage.)

JOHN DODGE. Isn't there something you can give me?

FEMALE DOCTOR. We have you on an anti-toxin named Neovitamole. *(brief pause)* This is just a precaution, but, is there anyone you want us to contact?

JOHN DODGE. *(pause)* Can you give me more of that stuff, just to make sure?

FEMALE DOCTOR. You're at the maximum. It's doing what it's going to do.

JOHN DODGE. What's it doing? What do I have?

FEMALE DOCTOR. I don't want to overwhelm you with details. You're showing signs of an infection, which we're trying to identify, and then, when we do, we can treat it.

JOHN DODGE. I'm having some trouble with my legs. And, my stomach's been… I've had diarrhea.

FEMALE DOCTOR. They told me. It can also strain the breathing, which is the big danger, if it's what we're worried about.

JOHN DODGE. It's curable, though, right?

FEMALE DOCTOR. We have high hopes on the Neovitamole. We'll see, fairly soon. It works quickly when it works. If not, there are other treatments. Some are somewhat radical, but they've been effective.

JOHN DODGE. What are they? No, forget it. You'll tell me when you tell me. *(brief pause)* What happens when you die?

FEMALE DOCTOR. You don't need to think about dying.

JOHN DODGE. But what happens? Do you think.

FEMALE DOCTOR. A few things. Dying, from the outside, from the bodily perspective, it's not very pretty. Nobody looks very peaceful, as far as I've seen. We have stories of people seeing white light and feeling an angelic serenity. But these are stories from the people who lived, so they might be just describing what it's like to almost die and then live. So we don't know. *(brief pause)* I was just speaking with a patient who's about to give birth.

JOHN DODGE. I guess that about covers it.

FEMALE DOCTOR. Those are just two events. There's a lot in between.

JOHN DODGE. I've always been afraid that shame would be the last thing I felt on Earth. No angelic stuff, no light – just weird pain, and shame that I was sick. And that I'd feel alone, no matter who was there. I've always been afraid of that. And now I just don't want to die like some dirty animal, with my teeth showing and some crazy look in my eye. *(brief pause)* I'm sorry to talk like this.

FEMALE DOCTOR. No, it's good. In fact, we have someone here who's wonderful. Once we clear up this other thing, I think it'd be good for you to meet with her. Just to talk.

JOHN DODGE. I'd like that. *(brief pause)* I guess this is a real irony. Me being here. How I got here.

FEMALE DOCTOR. Irony is a people thing. Nature is very frank. You're here, and we're taking care of you, is the point. Just this morning, my son Eric, he's seven, said, "The sun doesn't know it's hot, right? It just goes around being orange."

JOHN DODGE. I don't want to die. God. I don't want to be in a hospital.

FEMALE DOCTOR. It's going to be okay.

JOHN DODGE. Oh, it is? For who? *(He becomes nauseous.)* I'm getting this wave. I feel sick. I'm sorry. I think I'm going to be sick.

FEMALE DOCTOR. I can walk you to the bathroom, but it's better to stay still.

(She gets him a plastic bag.)

Use this, if you need it.

JOHN DODGE. Is this the medicine or the thing?

FEMALE DOCTOR. The nausea? It could be both.

JOHN DODGE. When is it supposed to... God...

FEMALE DOCTOR. Just try to relax. Try to breathe. We're doing everything we can do.

JOHN DODGE. I don't want to be here. I don't want to be sick. *(Brief pause. The nausea is passing.)* Okay. All right. I think I'm all right. Sorry. I'm sorry.

FEMALE DOCTOR. I'm going to get you something for your stomach. *(Referring to the call button by the bed.)* Ring if you need anything or if there's any change.

JOHN DODGE. I made a mistake.

FEMALE DOCTOR. Don't worry about that. Just think ahead. Think about simple true things.

JOHN DODGE. Okay. I'll try. The sun is orange.

FEMALE DOCTOR. That's the spirit. Think of good things. I'll come through again soon.

*(**FEMALE DOCTOR** exits.)*

JOHN DODGE. I'm thinking of good things.

*(**JOHN DODGE** covers his face with his hands, perhaps begins to quietly cry.)*

Scene Five

(Loading dock behind hospital. There are cardboard boxes and bags of garbage lying around. MECHANIC is looking through them, examining little bits of trash. FEMALE DOCTOR enters and stands on the raised loading dock.)

MECHANIC. Sorry. *(He begins to leave.)*

FEMALE DOCTOR. No, help yourself. I doubt there's anything good.

MECHANIC. I'm just looking around.

FEMALE DOCTOR. I used to smoke. I still come out here and just stand around for five minutes and think about cigarettes. Don't you volunteer, here?

MECHANIC. Yeah. I'm also a… I collect stuff.

FEMALE DOCTOR. Oh?

MECHANIC. Yeah. Just any kind of, like,… honestly, I'm basically looking for some pills or something. Do you think there's anything in here for a headache? A serious one?

FEMALE DOCTOR. I doubt it, no.

MECHANIC. Probably not. You look important, up there. Like a person who saves lives. Very, you know, sort of –

FEMALE DOCTOR. *(interrupting:)* I'm not going to give you any pills.

MECHANIC. Oh. You still look – you know – you look really professional.

FEMALE DOCTOR. Thank you. Careful you don't cut yourself. You can get botulism.

MECHANIC. That's a good name for a disease.

FEMALE DOCTOR. Isn't it. I always thought it sounded like a philosophy of really bad choices. People think it's not around anymore, botulism, but it is, it's alive and well.

MECHANIC. I'll be careful. *(brief pause)* Today's my birthday.

FEMALE DOCTOR. Happy birthday. *(nodding back toward hospital)* Someone's about to have a birthday in here.

MECHANIC. I guess it's pretty common. *(brief pause)* I was a perfect baby.

FEMALE DOCTOR. I don't think I've ever heard anyone say that.

MECHANIC. Yeah. I just... I was all ready. For the world.

FEMALE DOCTOR. Surprise.

MECHANIC. Yeah.

FEMALE DOCTOR. It's not rare, but, it's very lucky – to be a person, just a regular person. Did you know when you combine an egg cell and a sperm cell, there's more ways they can combine, more particular kinds of people that can result, than there are atoms in the Universe?

MECHANIC. I love facts like that. *(very brief pause)* I used to be seven pounds, eight ounces. Now look at me. *(brief pause)* I think I disappointed everybody when I was born. If they'd just been expecting a little animal that needed air and food, then I think I would've been pretty impressive. There was no way I could live up to all that want and need, me and my seven pounds, eight ounces. I think being born hurt my feelings. *(Still looking around.)* My head is killing me.

FEMALE DOCTOR. I'm sorry. *(brief pause)* Can I ask you, this'll sound silly, but, what do you want out of life?

MECHANIC. Are you kidding?

FEMALE DOCTOR. Just for fun.

MECHANIC. Okay. I want, out of life, for this headache to go away. And, then, just, I guess, to know something. At the risk of sounding like some fuck-up pawing through the garbage for drugs: I want to know Love. I want to calmly know love on Earth. And to feel beautiful.

(Pause. He starts looking around, again. No trace of amusement.)

Thanks. That was a lot of fun.

FEMALE DOCTOR. Pretty good answer. *(brief pause)* I ask people sometimes and they say they don't know. You'd think we'd take the time. We have answers for so many things. How many atoms in the Universe, how black holes are made. *(pause)* I'm sorry, I don't mean this to be embarrassing.

(She takes a vial of pills out of her jacket pocket, double-checks the label, then pours some on the ground.)

Sometimes people spill things, back here. You're not driving, are you?

(He shakes his head "no.")

Happy birthday.

MECHANIC. *(picking up the pills)* Yeah, you too. Thanks.

Scene Six

(Hospital room. **JOHN DODGE** *in bed.* **ATTENDANT 2** *enters and performs some routine task. She smiles at* **JOHN DODGE**, *who smiles back, as she exits.* **MRS. SWANSON**, *on a stroll down the hall, appears at the door.)*

MRS. SWANSON. John? I don't believe it.

JOHN DODGE. Mary. Hi. Wow. Let me sit up. *(He lifts himself up in bed.)*

MRS. SWANSON. *(laughing sympathetically:)* Oh, no. Look at you. What happened? *(She enters.)*

JOHN DODGE. A couple things. Look at you. I could ask you the same thing.

MRS. SWANSON. This is so funny. I kept thinking I'd see you.

JOHN DODGE. I know, me too. I was always looking. I thought I saw you a couple times.

MRS. SWANSON. I almost called when it was so rainy. Remember all that rain? Our basement flooded.

JOHN DODGE. I almost called you, a few times. I'd, I don't know, I had really thought we'd have more of a relationship.

MRS. SWANSON. Well, we did. We do.

JOHN DODGE. Not a relationship, but, I mean, just, I don't know, I thought I'd see you.

MRS. SWANSON. And, here I am. Ta da!

JOHN DODGE. I mean before. I guess I just thought we had a chance.

MRS. SWANSON. A chance of what?

JOHN DODGE. Oh, I don't know. Just a chance.

MRS. SWANSON. *(very brief pause)* Well, I guess we always do, right?

JOHN DODGE. You're nice. *(brief pause)* You're so big. You look really great.

MRS. SWANSON. Today's the day, I hope. What about you? Are you okay?

JOHN DODGE. Yeah, no, I'm fine, it's just something stupid. I cut myself.

MRS. SWANSON. Making a birdhouse or a canoe or something? One of your projects?

JOHN DODGE. No, just, I don't know, around the house.

MRS. SWANSON. Do you have a cold?

JOHN DODGE. Do I sound stuffed up? I think I'm just tired. Good place to get some quiet, anyway.

MRS. SWANSON. I don't know how quiet it'll be for me.

JOHN DODGE. Oh, you'll be great. It's really nice to see you. Wow. *(pause)* This is going to be dumb. Don't make fun of me.

MRS. SWANSON. What?

JOHN DODGE. *(trying not to cry)* Mary, sorry, can you hold me? Just for a – can I hold you?

MRS. SWANSON. I'm not sure how holdable I am. *(She sits on the bed.)* But I can give you a hug.

(They hug. It's comforting and possibly even romantic to **JOHN DODGE,** *nice but slightly uncomfortable for* **MRS. SWANSON.***)*

JOHN DODGE. Mary.

MRS. SWANSON. *(She sits on the bed, as before.)* It's good to see you.

JOHN DODGE. It feels really good to see you. The people are nice here, but I don't really know anyone. So is your husband here?

MRS. SWANSON. Can you believe it, he isn't. He's trying to get a flight, right now. *(She notices his bandaged wrist.)* Oh, no – you cut your hand? What did you do?

JOHN DODGE. It was stupid.

MRS. SWANSON. Oh, John – did you do this?

JOHN DODGE. Partly, yeah – I don't know. Yes.

MRS. SWANSON. Why? That's a stupid question, I'm sorry. But, why?

JOHN DODGE. A couple things. A lot of things. It was a mistake.

MRS. SWANSON. God. I wish I'd known. I don't know what I could have done, but... I just wish...

JOHN DODGE. Yeah. I wanted to call. I don't know what I would've said. But, I'm all right. *(brief pause)* If Bob doesn't make it, I can try to be there, in the delivery room. If you need someone.

MRS. SWANSON. That's really sweet. I don't want to be alone in there. *(brief pause)* It might not be good, though, because you're... if it turns out you do have a cold.

JOHN DODGE. Okay. But, I don't think I do.

MRS. SWANSON. It's really nice of you to offer. *(brief pause)* I'm sorry, I've got a lot on my mind.

JOHN DODGE. Yeah.

MRS. SWANSON. *(She gets up from the bed.)* It's so good seeing you. They said activity was good. I was walking up and down the halls.

JOHN DODGE. I know, I can't believe it. *(brief pause)* All these time. I mean, all these months.

MRS. SWANSON. The sink still drains like a dream. *(brief pause)* Remember you unclogged our sink?

(Long pause. He's dozed off. He opens his eyes.)

JOHN DODGE. *(quietly:)* Hey, Mary.

MRS. SWANSON. Hey. You need some rest. And, John, I should keep walking. They say activity is good.

JOHN DODGE. *(somewhat hazily:)* Sorry. God, I'm really tired. They've got me on this really serious stuff – it makes me so sleepy. *(very brief pause)* It's so great that... Good old Mary.

MRS. SWANSON. Rest up and I'll see you soon, all right? Oh, here's some news, wait until you hear, you'll love this: we think we're going to name him John.

JOHN DODGE. *(He hasn't heard.)* All right, Mary. It's really good to – I keep saying that, sorry. See you later, Mary.

(He begins to doze off again. She leaves the room.)

MRS. SWANSON. Did you hear what I – . Rest up. Bye, John.

(In the doorway, only partially visible to the audience, MRS. SWANSON *doubles over. In pain:)*

Oh. Sorry? I think this is… John, can you call someone? Can you ring your call thing? John?

(He's asleep.)

Someone? Somebody? I'm sorry, hello!?

*(*ATTENDANT *arrives, mainly out of view and out of earshot, and helps* MRS. SWANSON *off.)*

(Pause. JOHN DODGE *gets out of his bed. Stands, turns, and faces out. He reaches for the bed, and steadies himself with it.)*

JOHN DODGE. Was someone… hello? *(Brief pause. Quietly:)* Hey, I'm standing.

(Lights down.)

Scene Seven

(Entrance and lawn of Middletown Hospital.)

*(The tree is planted. **MECHANIC**, looking haggard, is sitting on a bench, staring at the pile of three rocks. He sips from a bottle in a paper bag. **LIBRARIAN** comes out of the hospital entrance.)*

LIBRARIAN. You've found a nice spot.

MECHANIC. *(referring to the rocks:)* I'm just looking at this.

LIBRARIAN. Maybe it's a sign.

MECHANIC. Maybe it isn't a sign. *(pointing to the sign that says emergency)* Maybe *this* is a sign.

LIBRARIAN. Maybe they're both signs. I'm here visiting a friend.

MECHANIC. I'm here, being difficult.

LIBRARIAN. You were always kind of a suspicious package. *(brief pause)* I remember when you were little. Remember that? You wrote an essay for Middletown Day called "This Whole Hamlet is Shaking." I had it hanging up at the library for years. I still remember the first sentence. "If this were..." no. "If Middletown was a horse instead of a town, it would be better for everyone and I would ride it off into the sun." Was that it?

MECHANIC. Wow. Yeah, that sounds right. It's always surprising when people remember something. I had to read it in front of everybody. I was shaking myself. It gave the thing an air of, like, I don't know – it made it more believable.

LIBRARIAN. I remember. They put your picture in the paper.

MECHANIC. Yeah. The color came out funny. All I was was the shape of a kid, with blurry teeth and hair.

LIBRARIAN. You could still tell you were happy. You looked very proud.

MECHANIC. I probably was. *(brief pause)* I think someone scared my mother, before I was born, a lot. So all the blood I got was shaky blood. Jumpy blood from my jumpy mother. And I want other people to enjoy the same experience. That's probably why I wrote that thing.

LIBRARIAN. I thought it was big of you. To stand up there and shake and say what you think and feel. We all have our ideas. Some people say the secret to life is being able to live in the middle of all our different ideas about life.

MECHANIC. Some people don't say anything.

LIBRARIAN. True.

MECHANIC. I didn't mean anything. Forget I said that.

LIBRARIAN. Okay. *(brief pause)* My mother used to sing "You Are My Sunshine" to me, at night. And then she'd sing, "Kentucky Moon," in the morning.

MECHANIC. That's nice. Mine was on her own. She tried, I think. Just bad luck, I guess. A world full of fathers out there, but try to find one when you need one. My father was a speech impediment, is how I usually think of him. He came by once with a doll and some wrong-sized clothes.

LIBRARIAN. My father was very tall. He felt that posture was very important.

MECHANIC. Oh, yeah? *(nodding towards the hospital.)* I forget, do they have food in there?

LIBRARIAN. There's a little snack bar. I had a good soup, the other day.

MECHANIC. It's weird. *(He takes a pill.)* I've taken a lot of these. It's weird to be alive. I know it's supposed to be really important and great. But, here's my philosophy. I'm sitting outside. I'm wearing this shirt and these shoes. It's this certain weather. This is my body, that's yours, end of story.

LIBRARIAN. I can't argue with that.

MECHANIC. Thank you. *(brief pause)* Is this all right?

LIBRARIAN. Of course. I'm just here, waiting.

MECHANIC. Can I ask, did anyone ever explain things to you? Other than stuff about posture? Like, like, really sit down and just say, "Okay, You: here's how this whole thing works"?

LIBRARIAN. *(brief pause)* There's an Indian prayer I always liked. I had it up on the wall, too. "If it's raining, it's not snowing. If it's snowing, the deer are thin. If the thin deer are sleeping, it is sunny. Hold the hand of your love and wait for the moon. Some things we are never to know. Listen to the brook." It's sort of woodsy, but, I always liked it. I don't know if I have it word-for-word.

MECHANIC. It's nice. "Listen to the river." That's good. We did Indians in school. I did a re-enactment. People clapped and my mom cried. That felt good. *(brief pause)* There're people like me in the world, I think. You don't hear much from us because we usually don't say anything. But we're out here, trying to get a hold on the whole thing. It's like, I don't know, it's like trying to fix a moving car.

LIBRARIAN. I think we're born with questions and the world is the answer.

MECHANIC. Yeah? I guess there're a lot of different ways to go. Some people love God. I have a neighbor who kayaks every weekend. *(brief pause)* You're not going to ask me what I want out of life, are you?

(**LIBRARIAN** *shrugs and smiles, and shakes her head, as if to say, "I don't know, should I?"*)

MECHANIC. *(Pause. Trying not to cry.)* I just wish I got somewhere, you know? That I was born, and then I grew, somehow. I'd like people to look at me and feel wonder. I'd like people to look at me and say, "Wow. Look at that guy." I'd like to look up at the sky and just think, "Hey, look at the sky." *(pause)* What kind of soup was it?

LIBRARIAN. Tomato. Did you ever think you might be a normal person?

MECHANIC. Maybe. I don't know. Bad news for normal people. *(brief pause)* I took a ton of those pills.

LIBRARIAN. Are you all right?

MECHANIC. Yeah.

(COP enters, from hospital entrance.)

COP. Hi, afternoon. *(to MECHANIC)* You again, on a bench, again, with your pupils all constricted. You're Craig, right?

MECHANIC. Did you get a call to come down here and strangle me?

COP. Why would – no. They want you in there.

MECHANIC. Why don't you like me?

COP. *(to LIBRARIAN:)* What's this?

LIBRARIAN. He's not feeling well. Be gentle.

COP. *(gently)* Okay. Craig, I'm sure you'll be fine. You've been really good about showing up for these. They want you in there, okay?

MECHANIC. Okay.

(He slowly gets up, begins to slowly enter hospital.)

(to LIBRARIAN:) Good luck with your friend. *(exits)*

LIBRARIAN. Bye, Craig. Thank you.

COP. I think he wrote the dirty word on the sign coming into town. I'm sorry, I never liked his attitude. Like he's always thinking there's somewhere better to be than here.

LIBRARIAN. Maybe there is. A lot of people probably feel that, sometimes.

COP. Maybe. Probably. Ah, God, I don't know – I'm sorry. I don't even know the guy. I guess I'm not feeling very patient.

LIBRARIAN. I'm sorry about your mother, Robert.

COP. Thanks, Judith. Thanks for coming.

LIBRARIAN. You made a beautiful speech.

COP. I didn't prepare anything. I thought I'd just go up there and talk.

LIBRARIAN. Well, it was lovely. Everyone cried and felt so close to her.

COP. I almost cried. I had a hard time not crying.

LIBRARIAN. You were a good son.

COP. *(brief pause)* They had her on every kind of drug, at the end, so she wasn't very clear. She did these things with her hands. My sister thinks she was playing piano in her mind. Remember she used to teach music? It made us happy to think that's what was happening, that she was playing some song in her head. We were happy she had things to do, even though there was nothing to do in there.

LIBRARIAN. It was good you could be with her. She was a wonderful woman.

COP. She was almost our oldest resident. *(brief pause)* A few days before, I was here visiting, and she asked me, "What does this actually mean?" and she held up her middle finger. It was so funny. I said, "Mom, where'd you see that?" It was on some show that had couples working out their problems. She couldn't work the remote to turn it off. But, so, I told her it means, "I don't like you." Then I felt so terrible, almost sick, for even saying those words to my mom, even though I was just explaining. I just wanted to get her flowers and make her laugh and help her get back home and feel peaceful.

LIBRARIAN. I'm sure she knew how you felt. That's a sweet story. *(pause)* People know what happens.

COP. Yes, they do.

LIBRARIAN. It seems so original, when it happens to us.

COP. I like the natural order of things, but, yeah, it's hard. When we were leaving, after, her doctor said, "See you later." My sister and I had a laugh about that, over breakfast. Yes, we shall. Sorry – how are you?

LIBRARIAN. I'm fine, thank you. Mary Swanson is supposed to be having her baby, today.

COP. From over on Oak Street, right? Number 31?

LIBRARIAN. Yes. Mary. That's funny – is that how you remember people?

COP. What? The address? Yeah, I guess. Just a habit. If I know the address, the general layout, then I can sympathize. *(brief pause)* Toward the end, I sat with my mom and we listed stores we'd been to. Isn't that sad, that one day, there's going to be a last store you ever went into?

LIBRARIAN. It is. But isn't it great to think there was a first? *(She thinks for a moment.)* Frank's Superette.

COP. Frank's Superette.

LIBRARIAN. *(brief pause)* Look at this pretty tree.

COP. Yeah. It's nice. I like trees. Everybody does, I'm sure, but, yeah, me too. *(very brief pause)* I should get back in here. Will you be at the library tomorrow?

LIBRARIAN. I will.

COP. I'll come in and say hi.

LIBRARIAN. I'll say hi, back.

COP. Thanks, Judith. Thanks.

(COP enters the hospital.)

Scene Eight

(**MRS. SWANSON**'s *hospital room.* **MRS. SWANSON** *is in bed.* **ATTENDANT** *enters with a pitcher of water.*)

ATTENDANT. *(doing some quick business, chart-checking, etc.)* Make sure you drink some water. Even if you're not thirsty.

MRS. SWANSON. Okay.

ATTENDANT. How are you? *(brief pause)* Can I get you anything?

MRS. SWANSON. Oh, sorry. No. Thank you. I was just thinking about everything.

ATTENDANT. Everything, wow. That's good to do, sometimes. And sometimes it's good to just look out a window. Everything's going to be fine. I'll be up again with some food in just a bit.

MRS. SWANSON. Food.

ATTENDANT. Not hungry?

MRS. SWANSON. I don't know. I'm just kind of... God.

ATTENDANT. You're kind of God? Very nice to meet you. I have a cousin who's a huge fan. It'll all come back, your appetite and everything. *(checking her forehead for fever)* Do you feel all right, otherwise?

MRS. SWANSON. I just thought everything would be different.

ATTENDANT. And it isn't?

MRS. SWANSON. People had trouble with travel arrangements. My husband and one of my brothers. Whatever was going to happen, I just didn't think I'd be alone.

ATTENDANT. They'll get here. Don't feel alone. You're not alone. Just rest. *(motioning toward a call button)* Ring, okay. If you need anything.

MRS. SWANSON. I will, thanks. (**ATTENDANT** *exits.*) I'm not alone.

Scene Nine

(JOHN DODGE's hospital room. JOHN DODGE is lying in bed. COP enters.)

JOHN DODGE. *(Somewhat scared and confused. His voice is slightly hoarse.)* I'm sorry. Am I not supposed to be –

COP. *(interrupting:)* It's okay. Hi. I'm Sergeant Hollingsworth. I don't know if you remember, I came to your house when the ambulance was there.

JOHN DODGE. Sorry, I thought I was in the wrong room. I remember. It was busy, but I remember you.

COP. I wanted to let you know there won't be any charges filed here. The arrangement is you'll do some community service when you get better and that you'll agree to get some help, some counseling.

JOHN DODGE. Thank you.

COP. Does that sound all right?

JOHN DODGE. Have you talked to them, here?

COP. No. Why?

JOHN DODGE. I don't know.

COP. Does it sound all right?

JOHN DODGE. Okay.

COP. *(He puts some papers by the bed.)* Look at these. They need to be signed. The address to send them to is up at the top. Are you feeling better?

JOHN DODGE. I think I'm losing my voice.

COP. Well, you were a real mess. *(brief pause)* You look better.

JOHN DODGE. Did you tell Stephanie?

COP. Who's Stephanie?

JOHN DODGE. I don't know. I'm sorry. She's from when I was little. *(brief pause)* I don't hear any voices in my head. Should I be hearing any voices?

COP. Are you all right?

JOHN DODGE. I think so.

COP. Just rest up and listen to your doctors.

JOHN DODGE. I will.

COP. Life can get tough. It's tough for everyone. You know that, right?

JOHN DODGE. Yeah.

COP. I get moody. I get sad. People don't think of cops as moody. *(gesturing toward his gun, notebook, flashlight, etc.)* Look at all this stuff I have to walk around with.

JOHN DODGE. It's a lot of stuff. *(brief pause)* I just want to be a regular living person.

COP. You will. I have to be back for something else, tomorrow. I'll stop in.

JOHN DODGE. Stephanie is from when I was little. I was little.

COP. Stephanie. Okay. *(brief pause)* I'll have them stop in and check on you, okay? Have a look at those papers and send them back.

JOHN DODGE. Are you leaving?

COP. Yeah, I've got to go. See you later.

JOHN DODGE. Okay.

COP. So, one part of the community service thing is managing the community garden on West Street. Building little stuff and just making sure everything's all taken care of. They said you're good with stuff like that.

JOHN DODGE. Yeah, I like stuff like that.

COP. Well, then, get better. I think they give you a uniform or something.

JOHN DODGE. That'd be good. I like working outside.

COP. All right, then. I'll see you later. *(exits)*

JOHN DODGE. Bye.

Scene Ten

(MRS. SWANSON 's room. MRS. SWANSON *sitting up in bed. Warm light.* FEMALE DOCTOR *enters with the tiny baby, swaddled in a blanket.)*

MRS. SWANSON. *(with nothing but love)* Ohhh.

FEMALE DOCTOR. *(She gently hands the baby to* MRS. SWANSON.*)* Somebody needs you.

MRS. SWANSON. I missed him so much. Was he fussing?

FEMALE DOCTOR. He just wants his mommy. *(She pulls up the blanket, to cover the baby, which makes a small sound.)* Take the cloth off him. There you go. As much skin-to-skin contact as possible. Just let him feel you holding him. Look at you both. You're like a Renaissance painting.

MRS. SWANSON. He feels so nice.

FEMALE DOCTOR. Everything's fine. He's a very healthy baby.

MRS. SWANSON. Oh, good. Lucky boy. My lucky healthy boy.

FEMALE DOCTOR. I'll leave you two.

MRS. SWANSON. Thanks, Julie. Thank you.

*(*FEMALE DOCTOR *exits.)*

(softly:) Johnnie. There you go. That's nice. Hello, John. Welcome to the world, little boy. How does it feel? I wonder what you're feeling. There you go. Ssshhh. What are you feeling on Earth?

Scene Eleven

(Follows quickly on Scene Ten. **JOHN DODGE***'s hospital room.* **JOHN DODGE** *is lying in bed. Occasional, and then building sounds of labored breathing. Suddenly, he goes into small convulsions. A muffled and very congested scream. This should all be protracted, irregular, underplayed, difficult to watch. He's dying like an animal. A desperate look toward audience and then he is still. Lights down.)*

Scene Twelve

(Follows quickly on Scene Eleven. **MRS. SWANSON** *and the body of* **JOHN DODGE** *are visible, though in darkness, on the stage. The playing area between them should be unspecific, empty.* **MECHANIC** *enters, dressed as a Chakmawg Indian, with headdress, war paint, bells attached to his boots. He quietly and slowly begins a ceremonial American Indian chant and a dance, in the tradition of the Apache or Sioux. At first, it's somewhat simple and even clumsy, the way a schoolchild might do a re-enactment, but it becomes haunting and beautiful and strange, both in melody and movement. It slowly builds in intensity and even wildness, as he becomes more possessed and more convinced of his expressiveness. He continues, to his physical and emotional limit. Brief pause.)*

*(*ATTENDANT *enters.)*

ATTENDANT. Craig?

MECHANIC. *(This line is spoken very quietly and indistinctly.)* I was beautiful.

ATTENDANT. Did you just say you were beautiful?

*(*MECHANIC *nods.)*

Well, then, I'm sure you were. Everything fits okay? *(Brief pause. He nods.)* You're going to be in pediatric, today. The kids love to see the Rain Dance. Just move around, ring the bells. I don't know if you did any of the reading I gave you? Just be spiritual. Don't use "to be" verbs. No is, was, or, will be. Too many tenses gets confusing. They're just kids. Keep it simple. You know? "It rain and children grow strong, like tree. Sun cross sky many time. Life never die. This land never die." Something like that. Sound good? They'll love it. Okay? *(brief pause)* Did you just wake up? Are you okay?

MECHANIC. Yeah.

ATTENDANT. Are you going to be all right? *(He nods.)* All right. You'll be great. They're just kids. Smile and go around in circles and they see the history of the world. They're just like us, except smaller. Okay?

MECHANIC. Yeah.

ATTENDANT. Okay. Me go do some filing. Me want leave early, play tennis, before sun go away. Thanks, Craig.

(She exits.)

(MECHANIC *moves downstage. Brief pause. As if a soliloquy.)*

MECHANIC. Me.

(Lights down.)

Scene Thirteen

(**JOHN DODGE**'s *hospital room. Lights up on the body of* **JOHN DODGE**, *under a sheet.* **ATTENDANT** *and* **ATTENDANT 2** *are taking care of the room, unplugging equipment, etc. Lights will remain up on the body, throughout the rest of the play.*)

ATTENDANT. The coroner is on his way.

ATTENDANT 2. Dr. Elliman? He's nice.

ATTENDANT. His son goes to school with my daughter.

ATTENDANT 2. *(referring to a file that's hanging at the foot of the bed:)* Does this stay with the patient?

ATTENDANT. Yeah.

ATTENDANT 2. It's so quiet.

ATTENDANT. I think bodies soak up sound. Listen. *(to* **JOHN DODGE**'s *body:)* We are in a room. You are a body. *(to* **ATTENDANT 2:**) Do you notice that? *(again, to* **JOHN DODGE**'s *body:)* This is the sound of my voice. This is the language I use. You are far away. Where are you? What are you feeling? *(Brief pause. To* **ATTENDANT 2:**) It sounds strange, doesn't it.

ATTENDANT 2. I guess. It's weird. Did you talk to him, before?

ATTENDANT. A little. He was worried about a library book. He was sad but he tried to be good-natured.

ATTENDANT 2. I came in once to change something and he said, "If I had flowers, I'd give them to you."

ATTENDANT. That's sweet.

(one last bit of business)

I think that does it.

(She checks a schedule.)

Now I think we have to go up to five.

(They exit. **ATTENDANT 2** *lingers by the door.)*

ATTENDANT 2. *(to* **JOHN DODGE**'s *body:)* Goodbye, person. That was nice about the flowers. I hope you're not sad.

Scene Fourteen

(**MRS. SWANSON**'s *hospital room. She is lying in bed with the baby on her chest, under the covers.* **LIBRARIAN** *is sitting by the bedside, gazing at the baby. There is a radio in the room.*

LIBRARIAN. Ohh. Look at his little mouth.

MRS. SWANSON. I know. I still can't believe it. That's your little mouth.

(**COP** *enters.*)

COP. *(quietly:)* Hello. Are you... is everyone dressed? Hi. Congratulations. I'm Robert Hollingsworth. Judith was telling me. I'm really happy for you. I'm over on Pine Street, near the river.

MRS. SWANSON. Thank you, Robert. I'm Mary Swanson.

LIBRARIAN. He's a beautiful boy. Just perfect. He's sleeping.

COP. That's the life.

MRS. SWANSON. Thank you for visiting. It's nice to have people.

(*small sound from the baby as she re-adjusts him on her chest*)

COP. Yeah, no, of course. I had to be down here, anyway.

(**SWEETHEART,** *who was in the Intermission Audience earlier, enters. Perhaps she enters from the actual audience, and climbs up on stage.*)

COP. Hello, sweetheart. How did you get up here? Are you lost?

SWEETHEART. No.

MRS. SWANSON. Do you want to look?

(**MRS. SWANSON** *folds back the blanket a little.* **SWEETHEART** *comes closer and leans in to look at the baby.*)

SWEETHEART. Hi.

MRS. SWANSON. He says, Hello. He says, How are you?

SWEETHEART. Fine.

LIBRARIAN. Well. This has been quite a day.

(**SWEETHEART** *takes a glance across the stage at the body of* **JOHN DODGE.**)

(*looking at the baby:*) Doesn't he look peaceful.

COP. Yeah. (*to* **MRS. SWANSON**:) Why don't we... we should let you be.

LIBRARIAN. Yes, you should rest up.

(**COP,** *exiting with* **SWEETHEART**:)

COP. Congratulations, again.

LIBRARIAN. There's a radio. Would you like some music?

MRS. SWANSON. That might be nice.

LIBRARIAN. I'll leave you this and you can find something.

(*She gives* **MRS. SWANSON** *a remote control.*)

Okay, darling. I'll see you tomorrow. (*She exits.*)

MRS. SWANSON. (*to the baby:*) Those were our neighbors. (*She turns on the radio. It's a program about science.*)

RADIO. "...with a mass more than three times the weight of the sun, of such gravity that it collapses into a black hole. The structure of a black hole is very simple. There is the surface, and the center, or singularity, from which no light can escape. If my friend Sally could watch from a safe distance beyond the event horizon and see me fall into a black hole, what would she see? Sally would see me falling, slower and slower. It would appear that I'll never quite reach the center. If I were waving, she would see me wave, slower and slower. "Bye, Sally."

(**JANITOR** *enters* **JOHN DODGE***'s room, rolling a large trash can on wheels. He empties the trash can at the foot of bed, and lines the trash can with a new trash bag.*)

For me, the fall would only take a short time. Years would pass, where she was. Eventually, it would look to her as if I had stopped, mid-fall. She would see my hand in the air, my flailing legs, my smile, all frozen – all motion would stop for her. This is because the light from me takes so long to escape. Finally, it will cease altogether. By then, Sally's great-great-grandchildren will be very old people. And I will still be falling, will still be waving good-bye. Next week, we'll visit with a giant tortoise who has an interesting story to tell, if he could speak. He's over a hundred years old! We'll also talk with a man and woman who doubt almost everything they've ever" –

(MRS. SWANSON *changes radio stations with the remote control. On the new station the last thirty seconds or so of the choral part of Beethoven's Ninth Symphony is playing. After about five or ten seconds,* ATTENDANT 2 *enters to refill a water pitcher.* ATTENDANT 2 *gives a little wave to the baby, and then exits.* JANITOR *is still doing some tidying up in* JOHN DODGE*'s room, perhaps noting on a clipboard that he has cleaned this room.* MRS. SWANSON *listens to the end, as* JANITOR *makes his way toward her room. A sedate female voice comes on.*)

That was the Symphonie Number Nine, in a recording from 1981 of the Philharmoniker –

(MRS. SWANSON *turns radio off.*)

(JANITOR *enters.*)

JANITOR. Evening.

MRS. SWANSON. Hello.

JANITOR. Don't mind me. *(He empties the trash.)* Wow, is that a baby?

MRS. SWANSON. This is "John."

JANITOR. Excellent. Congratulations.

MRS. SWANSON. Thank you.

JANITOR. John's a good name.

MRS. SWANSON. Thank you.

JANITOR. I guess they all are, when you think about it.

(a small sound from the baby)

Hey, he's trying to talk. *(last bit of janitorial work)* Is the temperature all right in here?

MRS. SWANSON. Yes, thank you, it's fine.

JANITOR. Good. Okay, see you later. *(He exits.)*

MRS. SWANSON. Bye. *(to baby:)* Say bye. Say bye-bye.

(A pause. Lights fade.)

End of Play